DIETLOF REICHE

Ghost Ship

From The Chicken House

This is a terrific thriller, a ghost story and a mystery, all rolled into one – it's the *perfect* book for a holiday, or just a cosy evening's entertainment. But don't be deceived, there are twists and turns a-plenty in this story.

Can you unravel the clever curse at the heart of *The Ghost Ship?* Do you dare?

Barry Cunningham
Publisher

DIETLOF REICHE

Ghost Ship

Chicken House

2 Palmer Street, Frome, Somerset BA11 1DS

First published in the USA in 2005
First published in Great Britain in 2007
The Chicken House
2 Palmer Street
Frome, Somerset BA11 1DS
United Kingdom
www.doublecluck.com

Cover design by Radio
Translated by John Brownjohn
Designed and typeset by Dorchester typesetting Group Ltd
Printed in the UK by CPI Bookmarque, Croydon, CR0 4TD

1 3 5 7 9 10 8 6 4 2

British Library Cataloguing in Publication data available.
Library of Congress Cataloging in Publication Data available.

ISBN 978 1 904442 84 4

For Rosemarie

PART ONE
THE BAY

FIRST PROLOGUE

The Cornish woodcarver Jacob Adams was having a lean year – as lean and unprofitable, he thought, as if the devil himself had a hand in it.

If Jacob Adams had been born two hundred and thirty years later, he would simply have thought business was bad.

The first six months of 1772 were nearly over, and his order book was barely half full. Worst of all, no one had commissioned him to carve a figurehead, and figureheads were his speciality. Jacob Adams carved them for ocean-going sailing ships. A figurehead bore the same name as its ship, was mounted on the prow, and gazed out over the vast expanse of ocean ahead. It guided the vessel through dangers of all kinds and protected it from sea monsters, storms and pirates.

Or so sailors believed.

The fact was, sailing ships in those days all too often fell victim to storms and pirates – even, perhaps, to sea monsters.

In spite of their figureheads.

But was that any reason why Jacob Adams should be short of work?

And then, out of the blue, a sea captain had appeared in his workshop – a giant of a man wearing a three-cornered hat and a waisted, knee-length coat. 'I need a figurehead for my new ship,' he announced. 'I've christened her the *Storm Goddess.*'

Storm Goddess? Rather an unlucky name for a sailing ship, thought Jacob Adams. Aloud, he said, 'A lucky name for a sailing ship, Captain.'

'I sail in three days' time.'

'Impossible.' Jacob shook his head. 'I can't carve you a figurehead by then.'

The towering sea captain produced a leather purse from his pocket. 'Five doubloons, each worth sixteen silver piastres.' And he counted out five gold coins on the work-bench.

Jacob Adams did some mental arithmetic. Five doubloons were about as much as he could earn in six months – even if times were good, which they weren't. 'Very well, Captain,' he said finally, 'I'll carve you a figure-head.'

He'd only have to carve the head, as he already had in stock a body with both arms folded on its chest. It had been left on his hands by a customer who'd gone bankrupt – an unpleasant affair, and one that he didn't care to dwell on. The figurehead had been made for a ship named *Fortuna*, after the goddess of good fortune, and Jacob had given her a beaming smile. He now proceeded to saw off her smiling head.

Next he carved the Storm Goddess's head. He gave her an aquiline nose, a tight-lipped, resolute-looking mouth, and hair that seemed to be streaming out behind her in a stiff breeze.

But how to attach the head to the body?

Jacob bored a deep hole in the headless neck. That done, he filled it with glue and hammered in a wooden plug, leaving half of it protruding from the neck. Then he bored a similar hole in the underside of the Storm Goddess's head.

And then, having made the second hole, he had an idea.

An artistic idea.

It was an idea that would later – very much later – deliver the giant sea captain and his crew from a terrible fate.

He decided to give the Storm Goddess a pair of eyes.

She already had some eyes, of course; he'd carved them, after all. But that was just it: they were carved. However much he sandpapered them, they would never acquire the glossy surface of a living creature's eye. He had often thought of using glass – in fact, he'd even bought some glass balls for that very purpose. But what was the use? If he simply gouged out two sockets and inserted the balls, the figurehead would goggle like a dead fish. Better to carve her some eyelids and attach the glass balls from the inside.

Well, why not?

Jacob Adams enlarged the hole in the underside of the Storm Goddess's head and chiselled away her wooden eyes, leaving the eyelids intact. Then he inserted two glass balls from the inside and glued them in place. He did this very carefully as no sea water must be allowed to seep in.

And then he had another idea – a practical one this time. Once he had glued the head to the body, no air would penetrate the cavity. Unable to dry out, the unseasoned timber would rot. The cavity had to be treated in some way. Anyone who had deposited five gold doubloons on Jacob Adams's workbench was entitled to a figurehead that would last for many years.

Jacob used salts of mercury for preserving timber, an expensive but effective method. He dissolved three and a half ounces of the chemical in a bucket of water, turned the head upside down, and poured the solution into the cavity.

The next day he emptied out the liquid that had not soaked into the timber, dried the cavity as best he could, and stuck the head on to the plug, first smearing the join between the neck and the body with glue. Then he gave the head several coats of paint.

No one would be able to tell that the head and the body hadn't been carved from a single piece of timber.

Last of all, Jacob painted the eyes: whites, irises, and pupils. He felt sure that the paint would stay on the glass for a long time to come. At least, he hoped so.

Then he stood back and surveyed his handiwork.

The Storm Goddess gazed at him boldly and resolutely, with eyes as shining as those of a living creature.

'You'll serve your purpose well,' said Jacob Adams.

Just *how* well, he never suspected.

But that was all to come later.

Much later.

Two hundred and thirty years later, to be precise.

ONE

Sunday lunchtime was always the worst.

That was when every table in the Seashell Restaurant was occupied and customers queued impatiently outside. They were mainly parents with young children, as usual, Vicki noticed as she hurried to the serving counter with a tray.

Vicki was twelve. She liked little children, provided they didn't rampage around, spill their drinks, and smear ketchup all over the tablecloths. Unfortunately, all the youngsters having lunch today seemed to be the kind who did.

What there *did* seem to be was a secret telephone network via which all the seaside holidaymakers with little children had agreed to meet for Sunday lunch at the Seashell.

'One large, one small, and two kids on twelve,' said Vicki.

Eileen nodded and keyed in the order. A buxom blonde, Eileen ran the restaurant and, now that Vicki's mother had remarried, the household as well. Vicki's father, who was the real boss, was in charge of the kitchen.

'One large' meant a fillet of plaice with new potatoes, melted butter and peas; 'one small' was obvious; and 'kids' meant fishfingers and chips. And ketchup. Which meant that Vicki would have to change the tablecloth later.

'Everything OK?' asked Eileen, and Vicki nodded. Eileen was all right. Vicki could go to her when she'd been given a bad mark in maths and didn't want Dad to know, or when she wanted to be shown the best way to put on nail varnish. Or even when she had problems with boys.

Vicki scanned the restaurant. 'Watch out for any customers trying to catch your eye,' Eileen had told her. 'Never look away, and always give them a nod to show you've seen them.' Vicki wasn't responsible for the whole restaurant, of course. Just three tables, in fact, but they seemed to hold a magical attraction for families with little children. She only worked weekends during the holidays, and her dad couldn't pay her like his other staff, or he'd be in trouble with the local authorities. All she'd done in the past was clear away the dirty plates. This summer, for the first time, she'd been allowed to wait at the tables properly under Eileen's supervision. Vicki was big for her age, and the heavily laden trays gave her no trouble.

'Miss!'

Vicki nodded and aimed a 'Coming right away' smile at table twelve. The two children, a girl and a boy, had started squabbling, but their glasses of orange juice were still upright. They were bored, and no wonder. The Seashell held no appeal for little kids, even though there wasn't another place like it in the world. Almost every square inch of the spacious restaurant's walls was lined with seashells. Large and small, smooth and fluted, white and coloured, dull and shiny, round and elongated. Shells from the North Atlantic and the South Pacific (most of them from the latter, Vicki had discovered). Each of the shells had been stuck to the wall with its curved side facing outwards: huge clamshells, tiny mussel shells, medium-sized cowrie shells, and tropical cockleshells of all kinds. Vicki had looked up seashells in an encyclopedia. There were more than six thousand different kinds, and most of them seemed to be represented in the Seashell. To quote the local tourist brochure, the restaurant was an 'attraction'.

And not only because of the seashells: there was also the carved wooden head on the end wall. Less of an attraction was the portrait of an eighteenth-century sea captain hanging opposite it. Painted in oils, it didn't amount to much, from an artistic point of view.

'One large, one small, and two fishfingers,' said Vicki, unloading her tray.

'Thanks,' said the father. 'Tell me, er . . . that head on the wall over there, who's it supposed to be?'

'No one special. It's part of an eighteenth-century figurehead. All we know is, it belonged to a sailing ship named the *Storm Goddess*.'

'And the man in the three-cornered hat?'

'That's the last captain of the *Storm Goddess*. She went down in a storm somewhere off the coast near here.'

'Mum, I want a Coke!'

'Me, too!'

'Two more orange juices,' said the mother.

Two hours later the restaurant was nearly empty. The Sunday afternoon cream-tea brigade would soon be turning up, but for the moment Vicki could relax. She did so leaning against the counter. 'Never sit down,' Eileen had told her. 'If you absolutely must, doze on your feet. Only waitresses in fifth-rate burger bars sit down.' Vicki looked up at the figurehead. 'Hi, Storm Goddess,' she said, under her breath, of course – she didn't want anyone thinking her strange – but the Storm Goddess was a favourite of hers.

Vicki found the seashells interesting, and the captain too, but the carved head on the wall really fascinated her.

The Storm Goddess had been mounted on a kind of slanting base so that she leaned forward and looked down into the restaurant. But she didn't just look down, she looked straight at you.

The Storm Goddess was looking at Vicki – gazing sternly into her eyes as if guarding some secrets.

One of which Vicki knew.

As a little girl she'd thought that the Storm Goddess's gaze was meant for her alone, and that it followed her all around the room. This scared her until Dad mentioned that the figurehead seemed to be looking at him too. It was due to a peculiarity of the eyes: the Storm Goddess had a squint.

It was only a slight squint, and you wouldn't have noticed it unless you looked very carefully. More importantly, you couldn't tell *why* she was squinting, not from floor level. Vicki had found this out by chance. They'd been hanging up Christmas decorations, and a big ladder had been leaning against the wall beside the Storm Goddess. Although Vicki's father had strictly forbidden her to climb it, she'd scrambled up while no one else was around. That was when she discovered that some of the paint had flaked off the Storm Goddess's right eye, just beside the black pupil. She also saw that the eye was made of glass.

Vicki had told no one of her discovery. It had remained a secret between her and the Storm Goddess.

She looked up at the head on the wall, and the head returned her gaze. The Storm Goddess looked down at her gravely, as if to say, 'That's not the only secret I know.'

It was true. For instance: why was her head the only thing that was left of her? Figureheads were carved from a single piece of timber, but after the storm had sunk her ship, all that the waves had washed ashore was a head without a body. What had happened on board? Why had the head become detached from the body?

The history of the town, a big fat volume preserved in the public library, contained an account of the terrible storm that had raged in the autumn of 1772. However, all it said about the head was that it had been found on the beach and identified as belonging to the *Storm Goddess*. Reported to have been washed up at the same time was a packet wrapped in sailcloth and waterproofed with pitch. What had the packet contained?

Vicki continued to gaze at the Storm Goddess. What had happened to her out at sea? What had her eyes seen?

'Excuse me!'

Table twelve was now occupied by another couple and

their son, a boy of about Vicki's age with dark hair and black-framed glasses; the Harry Potter glasses with little round lenses. Vicki usually thought they looked stupid, but they looked OK on this boy. In fact, they suited him perfectly. She went over to the table.

'Are you the waitress?' The man looked her up and down. He was wearing an open-necked shirt and a gold chain around his neck. His wife, who looked bored, was slim and sunbed-tanned. She wore more gold jewellery than her husband – considerably more.

'You can't be any older than thirteen,' said the man.

'I look young for my age.' This was Vicki's standard response to remarks like that. Why did people like this come here on holiday? They belonged at a resort on the Costa del Sol. The boy looked nice, though. He smiled at Vicki, and she smiled back.

'Besides,' Vicki went on, 'I'm only doing this until I can go to maritime college. I aim to become a ship's captain.' She always added that for especially irritating customers.

'Some hope,' said the man.

The boy grinned.

'Peter,' said his mother, 'stop smirking.'

'OK,' replied the boy named Peter. His grin persisted. Vicki grinned back.

'Harry,' said the woman, 'let's go. I'd rather have a snack

21

by the swimming pool.'

Peter stopped grinning. 'Oh no, not again!'

'So this is the famous Seashell Restaurant.' His father surveyed the room. These people definitely belonged in Spain, Vicki told herself.

'Look, Peter,' the man went on, 'we came here on holiday because it's what *you* wanted. That's fine, but your mother and I would like to do some sunbathing – if the sun ever shines here. If you want to stay and eat, nobody's stopping you. Right?'

Peter looked at Vicki and nodded.

His parents got up and left.

What now?

'Can I bring you something to drink?' Vicki asked, blushing despite herself.

Peter nodded. 'A Coke?'

'Right away,' she said. She only hoped he hadn't noticed her blushing.

'Eileen,' she whispered when she reached the serving counter, 'you see that boy at table twelve?'

'What? Speak up. Which boy?' Eileen asked loudly.

Vicki wished she could sink through the floor, but it refused to swallow her up.

Eileen came to her rescue. By now she had spotted Peter and noticed that Vicki's face was as red as a tomato. 'Sit him down at number nineteen,' she said, lowering her voice.

This was a small, secluded table near the counter. It commanded a good view of the restaurant and was close to where Vicki relaxed – on her feet, of course – when she wasn't actually waiting at tables.

She gave Eileen a grateful nod.

'That sea captain story of yours was really funny.' Vicki had brought Peter his Coke, and he'd gathered that she couldn't join him at the table.

'I wasn't joking,' she said, leaning against the counter. 'It's what I really want to be.' She knew that it was unusual to have decided what she wanted to do so young. None of the other girls in her class seemed to worry about the future. She hesitated. Then she said, 'How about you? Any idea what you want to be?'

He nodded. 'A scientist. Physics or chemistry.'

Physics and chemistry certainly had nothing to do with the way her cheeks had started burning again. At least she sounded OK when she said, 'Why did you want to spend your holiday here?' Seeing the look on his face, she added quickly, 'Just curious.'

'Why *not* here?' Peter adjusted his glasses with his fore-finger. He'd already done that more than once – an appealing gesture, Vicki thought. She could imagine him fiddling with his glasses like that when he was reading. 'The thing is,' he went on, 'I didn't want to go on yet another beach holiday with my parents. Blazing sun, blue sea, white sand, blue pool, and – just for a change – a few green palm trees. It's so boring. That's why I chose somewhere different for my birthday: a proper old fishing village with tides that go in and out – maybe even some storms. A place where there are things to see.' He surveyed the restaurant. 'A room lined with seashells, for instance.'

'How did you know about us?'

'Some travel brochure. There was a photo, and the caption said that the Seashell Restaurant was worth a visit. But that wasn't what decided it for me.'

'It wasn't?' What bigger attraction did the town have to offer?

'No. There are seashells in Spain, too, plenty of them. What I found really interesting about the photo was that.' Peter pointed to the end wall.

'Waitress!'

So the Storm Goddess had lured him here!

'*Waitress!*'

Vicki was in demand again.

The restaurant had filled up. Vicki managed to exchange a

few more words with Peter and let him know, in passing, that she was the owner's daughter, but it was a while before she got the chance to go and stand beside his table again.

Peter hadn't been the least bit bored. He seemed to be the kind of boy who didn't always have to be the centre of attention; he could sit still and simply observe what was going on around him. At one point he produced a miniature telescope from the pocket of his jeans and surveyed the restaurant with it. Vicki, who noticed this as she bustled past, thought it was a bit odd. The telescope was now lying on the table in front of him.

'I read in the brochure that the *Storm Goddess* went down off the coast near here,' he said to Vicki, who was leaning against the counter again. 'Why is part of her figurehead here? I mean, why not in a museum?'

'I can explain that.' Vicki drew a deep breath. Explanations weren't her strong point. She looked at Peter, who was waiting expectantly. She told him that this had once been the *Storm Goddess*'s home port, and that her captain came from the town, like the first mate and some of the crew. And that the captain had been the owner, not only of the *Storm Goddess*, but also of the Seashell Restaurant.

Peter nodded. 'So that's why the head is here.' He stared at it some more and abruptly reached for his telescope again. Vicki sighed. Evidently, all boys had a craze for something, and Peter's seemed to be his stupid telescope. He withdrew his hand. 'And now it belongs to you.'

Vicki shook her head. 'We only rent this place from the harbour master.'

'The harbour master?'

'Yes, he's a direct descendant of the ship's captain. That's why he's the owner.'

'Oh.' Peter looked at the telescope again.

'But,' Vicki said quickly, 'the first mate of the *Storm Goddess* was an ancestor of *ours*.'

He looked up. 'Really? You're descended from an eighteenth-century sailor? Awesome.' His eyes strayed once more to his stupid telescope. 'Well,' he said, 'I'm no expert, but I think that head is pretty amazing. They ought to mention something as unusual as that in the brochure.'

'Mention what? What are you talking about?'

'The fact that the Storm Goddess's eyes are made of glass.'

TWO

Vicki stared at Peter.

She stared at him as if he were a conjuror who'd just told her she had three pounds in her pocket, even though she was clutching them tightly in her hand inside the pocket and there was no way he could possibly have known.

He *did* know it!

But how? It was her discovery, and she'd never mentioned it to a living soul. 'But . . . how did you know?'

'With that.' Peter pointed to his telescope.

Of course!

Vicki decided that perhaps miniature telescopes weren't so stupid after all.

'Like to see?' He held it out.

She shook her head. 'Not now. Anyway, I know what the

eyes look like.' And she told him how she'd found out, and that she'd never let on to anyone.

'Well, now I know, too.'

Did she mind? A little bit, she had to admit. She and the Storm Goddess had shared a secret, and now an outsider had butted in. Yes, she *did* mind.

'Do you know what that means?' asked Peter.

'Huh?' Vicki shook her head. 'What what means?'

'Look at the eyes: they must have been inserted from the inside. That means the head is hollow.'

Vicki didn't understand at first, then it dawned on her: if the head was hollow, something might be hidden inside it! There didn't have to be, of course, but there *might* be. She looked up at the Storm Goddess. Was *that* her real secret?

'I wonder,' said Peter, who was also looking up at the head, 'if there's something hidden in it?'

Vicki and Peter stared at each other. At last Peter said, 'Wouldn't *that* be something?'

Two minds with a single thought . . .

'Excuse me!'

Vicki had to go. She didn't always hate helping in the restaurant, but at that moment she did.

It was late afternoon, and the cream-tea brigade had disappeared.

So had Peter, unfortunately.

'I mustn't be too late getting back to the hotel,' he'd said. 'My parents aren't as stupid as they look. Sometimes they like to show who's boss.' He hesitated. Then he said, 'See you tomorrow?'

Vicki shook her head. 'Tomorrow's Monday. It's our day off.'

'See you Tuesday, then.'

It wasn't until later that Vicki suddenly realized how silly she'd been. What did 'day off' mean? A day off for the waitresses and kitchen staff, but not for her! She could easily have made plans with him for tomorrow, and she hadn't asked the name of his hotel, or his last name, or even his mobile phone number. What had she been thinking of?

Standing beside table nineteen, she looked up at the Storm Goddess. She and Peter had talked some more before he'd had to go. If something really was hidden inside the head, how could they get at it? Peter had wondered if Vicki's father would let them examine the head. 'No way,' she'd told him. How about secretly taking the head down at night? 'No way.' She'd reeled off one 'No way' after another until the situation became clear: *if* there was something hidden inside the Storm Goddess's head, it would remain her secret for ever. Vicki heaved a sigh.

'Busy day today, wasn't it?' Her father was standing in the kitchen doorway. Snow-white chef's hat, snow-white shirt and apron, grey trousers. He was a stickler when it came to dressing correctly, both inside the kitchen and out. His one piece of self-indulgence was a dark, stubbly beard. 'If the work gets too much for you, tell me, all right?'

Vicki nodded. 'I will, but it won't.'

Her father indicated the table beside her. 'Has he already gone?'

She nodded again. Of course Dad knew about Peter. Eileen kept him up to date about everything that went on in the restaurant.

'Seemed like a nice boy?'

'Mmm,' was all she said. What else could she say? But Dad would go on probing unless she gave him a few crumbs of information. Maybe this would do: 'He wants to be a scientist. His parents are a bit of a drag.' He kept looking at her, so she added, 'He'd seen a brochure with a picture of this place. That's why they came.' That ought to do, she thought.

Her father nodded. 'I see. Well, I'd better get on.' He turned to go. 'By the way,' he said over his shoulder, 'there's a chap coming to fetch the Storm Goddess tomorrow.'

It didn't sink in at first. With an effort, Vicki tried to make sense of what she'd just heard.

'*What* did you say?'

'Someone's coming to fetch the Storm Goddess tomorrow.'

'But . . . why? What for?'

She could hear that she sounded almost angry.

'Victoria!' That was what her father called her when he was cross, but also when he didn't know what to make of her. 'An expert on old woodcarvings is picking her up. He says she needs restoring.'

Vicki pulled herself together. 'Why didn't anyone tell me?' she asked quietly.

'I just have, haven't I?' He was looking almost guilty. 'I forgot, all right?'

Forgot? Vicki had her doubts. She'd long suspected her father of keeping certain things from her, one of them being the fact that the first mate of the *Storm Goddess* had been an ancestor of theirs. She'd learned that from her grandmother. Vicki felt sure that, for some reason, her dad didn't want her to know all there was to be known about the Storm Goddess. 'How did this expert know the head needs restoring, anyway?' she asked.

'He came a few weeks ago – one morning when you were at school. He discovered that the eyes are made of glass, and that it's probably hollow. Well, now I really must get going.' And he strode back into the kitchen.

Vicki sank into one of the chairs at table nineteen. She alone had shared a secret with the Storm Goddess for years. And now, all at once, at the end of a Sunday like any other, she was positively surrounded by other people who knew it too.

OK, so there were only three of them besides herself – up to now, at any rate. But it didn't matter whether there were three or three hundred. The secret wasn't a secret any more.

She looked up at the Storm Goddess.

The Storm Goddess gazed back at her, stern and tight-lipped. What other secrets was she harbouring? Whatever their nature, they were now in danger of being discovered.

Vicki drew a deep breath. 'Storm Goddess,' she said, 'I'm going to keep an eye on you.'

Vicki was up early the next morning.

Also quite early on the scene were two workmen, who proceeded to erect some scaffolding against the wall below the Storm Goddess. This was to help the expert on old woodcarvings to remove the head more easily. Except that the expert was late. The men from the scaffolding firm, who had really been meant to help him transport the head to his workshop, announced that they had another job to do and left.

Lunchtime came, then afternoon.

Vicki spent the whole day sitting in the Seashell, reading or watching the two women whose job it was to give the place a thorough clean once a week. 'Why not get some fresh air?' her father suggested, but she shook her head. The Storm Goddess was depending on her.

Finally, at about five o'clock, a little man in a beret and a painter's smock appeared. Vicki was the only person in the restaurant, so he introduced himself to her. 'Pacino's the name. I'm the antiques restorer. Sorry I'm late, but I had an angel to deal with in the next town.'

Mr Pacino obviously rated angels more highly than storm goddesses. Vicki told him who she was. Then she said, 'My father says something needs repairing. What, exactly?'

'So you're interested in eighteenth-century wood-carvings, are you, young lady?' The little man gave a condescending chuckle, but Vicki eyed him so sternly that he quickly suppressed it. 'Well, for a start, I'll have to replace the paint that's flaked off. On the eye, for instance.'

Vicki nodded. Just as she'd feared. Then the Storm Goddess wouldn't squint or appear to be watching her any more. Still, she could soon put that right.

'But the most important thing,' Mr Pacino went on, 'is to preserve the timber. The head must be hollow. Nobody

33

knows what it looks like inside.' He fell silent. Then he said, 'The timber may have started to rot.'

Vicki stared at him. That meant . . .

'That means the head could disintegrate at any moment.'

The Storm Goddess might disintegrate – and, with her, whatever might be hidden inside!

'I need to stabilize it as soon as possible.'

Again, Vicki stared at him in silence.

'Stabilizing it means preserving it, making it last,' he explained.

Vicki knew that, but she never could have guessed that, one day, she would fervently hope that a little man in a beret and a painter's smock really knew his job.

Vicki fetched her father from his office, where he'd been planning the restaurant menu for the week. She was now standing underneath the scaffolding, fidgeting with impatience, while her father and the expert were taking their time above her head.

'You hear that?' Mr Pacino tapped one of the big cockleshells on the restaurant wall with his knuckles.

'Of course,' said Vicki's father. 'It sounds hollow.'

'It's hollow, yes, but can't you hear a rattling noise?' Mr Pacino gave the shell another tap.

'Now I can. What is it?'

'Loose plaster, I should imagine. The shells were embedded in the plaster when it was still wet, and now they're coming loose.'

'Which means?'

'Which means that someday in the not-too-distant future they'll start falling off your walls.'

Vicki's father rubbed his bristly chin. He didn't raise his voice, but the rasping sound told Vicki that he was angry. 'In that case they'll be falling off the harbour master's walls, not mine. I only rent this place.'

'I heard you wanted to buy it.'

'I still do, but the harbour master refuses to sell.' Vicki's father rubbed his chin again. 'Pure spite, if you ask me.'

'Well, er . . . anyway, the whole place is in urgent need of restoration,' said Mr Pacino. 'And now I'll see to our patient.'

It was about time. Vicki had been tying her legs in knots to prevent herself from hopping up and down with impatience.

She waited for Mr Pacino to climb the ladder propped against the scaffolding, then asked quickly, 'May I come up?'

The little man paused. 'Why not?' he said. 'Perhaps you can give me a hand.'

Vicki climbed up and joined him on the platform.

'Can we call the scaffolders now?' her father asked from below. 'I want that scaffolding removed before the day's out.'

Mr Pacino nodded, and Vicki's father disappeared in the direction of his office.

Vicki was now as close to the Storm Goddess as she had been that Christmas – even closer, in fact. She could not only see where paint had peeled off the right eye, but could make out the thin cracks between eyelids and eyeballs from which Peter and Mr Pacino had deduced that the eyes had been inserted from within and that the head must be hollow.

'Hmm,' said Mr Pacino as he examined the head. 'It shouldn't be too difficult.' He turned to Vicki. 'Could you fetch me a blanket? It needn't be clean, just soft.'

Soft, naturally, but only a clean one would do for the Storm Goddess. Vicki raced down the ladder and up to her room, where she yanked a thick blanket from the drawer beneath her bed. Moments later she was back up the ladder and draping the blanket over the platform.

'You take the right side, I'll take the left,' Mr Pacino told her. 'Grip it by the chin and hair. Now wiggle it a bit . . . now lift it carefully at an angle. Yes, that's right.'

The head was surprisingly light. As they slowly raised it, Vicki saw that it had been resting on a thick wooden plug set into the base that supported it. 'And now, gently lower it down,' said Mr Pacino. 'Yes, that's right.' They laid the Storm Goddess on the blanket. 'Well done, young lady.'

Vicki merely nodded. Crouching down, she peered into the opening in the Storm Goddess's neck. Try as she might, she couldn't see a thing.

'Now for the moment of truth,' announced Mr Pacino. He produced a torch from a pocket in his smock and shone it into the hole in the neck. 'Hmm,' he said. Laying the torch aside, he produced a thin rubber glove from another pocket and put it on. Then, staring tensely ahead, he groped around inside the Storm Goddess's head. After a while he withdrew his hand and looked at it, then inserted it again.

Vicki couldn't restrain herself any longer. 'Well?' she demanded. 'What's inside there?'

'It's all quite sound,' said Mr Pacino, withdrawing his hand once more. 'No sign of rot. Someone must have used a highly effective preservative. A solution of mercury, probably.'

'Yes, but . . . isn't there anything inside? I mean, there must be.'

The little man stared at her in surprise. 'Like what?'

A secret, Mr Pacino. The Storm Goddess's secret, that's all.

*　　*　　*

Mr Pacino had climbed down the ladder and disappeared into the office to report to Vicki's father.

Vicki kneeled in front of the opening and peered in. There *had* to be something in there!

The interior of the head wasn't completely dark; light was getting in somehow. Not much, but some. Where was it coming from? Vicki suddenly grasped the truth: the light was coming in through one of the eyes. The right eye, where the paint had peeled off.

And then she could make out some lines on the inside of the head, just on the side of the cavity facing the eye. Not only lines, but grey and black splotches, as if someone had burned a picture into the wood. No, etched it. What could it be?

Of course, it might just be the grain of the wood or something.

Or *something*.

Vicki stared into the cavity. It was too dark inside. Her torch, she must fetch her torch. She'd better be quick, too, before the scaffolders came and Mr Pacino took the head away. She scrambled down the ladder.

'All right, that's what we'll do.' Her father emerged from his office accompanied by little Mr Pacino.

At that moment, there was a knock on the front door of

the restaurant. The men from the scaffolding company.

She had run out of time.

Vicki slowly sat down at table nineteen. The Storm Goddess was being taken away, and her secret with her.

There was *something* inside the head, she felt sure of it.

But she'd missed her chance.

'It's getting late,' said Mr Pacino. 'And since there's no real urgency, given the excellent condition of the timber, I'd prefer to leave it here for the time being.'

Leave *what* here?

'No problem,' said her father. 'It'll be safe enough in our storeroom.'

'Good. After two hundred and thirty years, you know, a head like that is a rarity. I'll be back to collect it in the next few days.'

Vicki rose to her feet.

The Storm Goddess wasn't being taken away after all! She was going into the storeroom!

The Storm Goddess was staying, and Vicki would be able to get to the bottom of her secret.

That very night.

THREE

The Storm Goddess had been locked up in the attic. Mr Pacino had condemned the storeroom as unsuitable: 'Cans of paint? Solvents? All that dangerous stuff on the shelves? No, I couldn't take the risk.' So the men from the scaffolding company had carried the head upstairs to the attic, which contained such harmless objects as an old trunk, a few rickety chairs and a discarded restaurant table. A woollen blanket was draped over the table, and the head deposited on top. Vicki's father locked the attic door and put the key in his pocket.

Later he told Vicki, 'Don't touch that head, will you? If anything happens to it, the harbour master will make us pay through the nose.'

Vicki nodded. Of course she'd be careful to see that

nothing happened to the Storm Goddess.

Like her father and Eileen, Vicki had a passkey that would open every room in the building, the attic included. But she would have to wait until late that night to go and look at the head again, when her father was asleep in his bedroom. And Eileen tucked up in hers.

In the meantime, maybe she should pay her grandmother a visit. She could look at her jewellery – she liked doing that. Glitzy earrings from India, bead necklaces from Africa, coloured bangles from the local department store – Gran always had something new for her to look at. Recently she'd shown Vicki a magnifying glass that she'd been using to read the newspaper. 'Not for much longer, though,' she'd said. 'I'm going to have those cataracts done.'

But then Vicki remembered Gran played bridge with her friends on Monday nights, and it was no fun sitting there while they slapped their cards down on the table and gossiped about things that meant nothing to her.

Why not go for a walk? It was only seven o'clock, and the sun hadn't set. Besides, the tide was out, and people would be strolling around on the mud flats.

Peter . . . maybe he was strolling around there too. Bound to be!

Vicki sensed this as strongly as if a telepathic message had winged its way to her.

The Seashell was on a small street just off the quay, and Vicki reached the slipway in no time. Stretching away in front of her, still in bright sunlight, was the famous, semi-circular bay that tourists came to see. As usual when the tide was out, the landward half of the bay was dry and the other half a watery expanse. The line between land and water ran straight across the bay as if drawn with a ruler. When the tide came in, the whole bay filled with sea water, right up to the sandy beach on one side and the quay on the other. But now, at low tide, only half of the bay was sea and the other half mud flats.

People were roaming across the mud flats. Most of them were paddling with their trousers rolled up and backpacks on, many with children. It looked as if the secret telephone network had been in action yet again, and that all the couples had arranged to meet up on the mud flats. No bigger than ants when seen at this distance, the children were messing around, yelling and jumping into the pools of black sludge left behind by the tide. Vicki could hear their shouts from where she was standing.

Where was Peter? She screwed up her eyes. She could make out the kids romping around in the mud and the grown-ups with their backpacks.

But none of the figures belonged to Peter – or not as far as she could tell. If only she'd had his telescope it would have been easy to spot him. But if she'd had his telescope, he'd have been right beside her, and she wouldn't have needed it . . . why couldn't that telepathic message have given a more specific location? Maybe that wasn't the point of such messages. She decided to walk along the quay.

If she turned left she would pass the school, then the town hall and police station. The road continued alongside the beach and turned inland just before the lifeboat station. Behind the lifeboat station was a fish and chip stand. She could stop there and have a chat with Phil, the owner. If she turned right she would come to the harbour – not that much was going on there at the moment. True, there was a channel that led across the bay from the harbour to the open sea, but only small fishing boats and motorboats could navigate that at low tide. Really big yachts – if they came here at all – had to anchor outside the bay. Things had been different in the *Storm Goddess*'s time. The harbour and the channel must have been far deeper than they were now. The local museum owned a print dating from those days. It showed four ocean-going ships, one of which was a three-decker, a pretty formidable warship. The oarsmen in the rowing boats must have found it quite an effort to tow such a large vessel into port. Once a ship had made it into the bay, however, she was safe from the very worst of storms. The *Storm Goddess* hadn't made it.

Vicki suddenly lost all desire to head for the harbour. She turned left instead. She was more likely to find Peter there anyway. On the left-hand side of the bay, just on the edge of the crowded little town, the luxury hotels nestled into the hillside, their enormous windows looking out towards the harbour. Peter and his parents were bound to be staying at one of them, since none of the guest houses in town boasted a swimming pool.

Vicki kept her eye on the mud flats as she made her way along the top of the quay. Still no sign of Peter anywhere. Just as she was passing the school, some music rang out from the square in front of the town hall. Old Captain Ahab and his 'band' – trumpet, accordion, drums – were about to set off on their Musical Mystery Tour of the mud flats. Maybe Peter would be going with them? Vicki broke into a run.

Captain Ahab's Musical Mystery Tours were another local attraction, according to the tourist brochure. After meeting up outside the town hall, the holidaymakers would follow him and his band all the way across the mud flats to the water's edge. Between tours there were balloon-blowing contests for the children, or dancing the hornpipe for their parents, or whatever else was on Captain Ahab's programme for the day. The tourist brochure boasted that these tours had been going for a hundred years – not that Captain Ahab was quite that old yet. He set off just as Vicki got to the town hall, followed by a crowd of expectant tourists. Vicki quickly scanned their ranks, but Peter wasn't there. She was disappointed in one way but relieved in another. Somehow, Peter and Captain Ahab didn't go together.

Vicki walked on. She turned off the road into a slipway by the lifeboat station, and there behind it stood Phil's fish and chip stand. It wasn't really a stand, just a trailer you could have towed behind a car, except that Phil had jacked it up on bricks and removed the wheels. He'd also fitted it with a big side window and a kind of counter. In front of the trailer were some open-air tables at which his customers could stand while eating their fried fish. But no one was standing at the tables now, nor at the counter. Through the side window Vicki could see Phil was in his den. He had fair, almost white hair and didn't look much older than Vicki herself, although he had to be over twenty.

'Hi, Phil,' said Vicki. 'How's it going?'

Phil came to the window. 'Badly,' he said drily.

Vicki laughed. She liked Phil and his fish and chips. He'd cracked his skull in a bad motorcycle accident some years earlier and had left school shortly afterwards. A lot of people in the town thought he was a bit slow, but he wasn't.

'That's because everyone's on the other side of the lifeboat station,' Phil went on, 'and I'm not allowed to operate there.'

He'd asked permission from the town hall to set up his trailer on the beach, but his application had been declined because, according to the harbour master, the beach and the mud flats were protected areas. Not even Phil's uncle, Inspector Tom Grogan of the local police, could help. 'It'd be against the law,' he told Phil. 'You know what the law is, don't you?' Inspector Grogan was one of those who thought Phil was stupid.

'I suppose you haven't seen a boy come past here?' Vicki asked. 'He wears little round glasses.'

'With black frames?'

'That's the one!'

'Then I haven't seen him. The one I saw had glasses with red frames.'

Vicki sighed.

It wouldn't get dark for a couple of hours yet.

On his day off Vicki's father usually went to bed early, which meant around eleven. Vicki, whose bedroom was

46

next door to his, was sometimes woken up long after that because Dad was still tossing and turning in there. A man who seldom got to bed before two a.m. six days a week could hardly be expected to go to sleep three hours earlier than usual on the seventh.

Tonight, however, all sounds from next door ceased shortly after eleven. It was as if some mysterious power had conspired with Vicki to make her father especially tired. But that, she told herself, was just a silly idea of hers.

Could she risk it yet? She tiptoed to the door and opened it a crack.

Silence reigned. Not a sound from anywhere in the building. Nothing to be heard but the murmur of the waves. The tide was coming in.

Vicki went over to her desk. Putting a torch in one pocket and her passkey in the other, she turned towards the door again. Wait! What if Dad was only pretending to be asleep? Was it a trap? Had he seen her experimenting in the hall and on the stairs to find out which floorboards creaked? No, he'd have said something right away. She was being stupid. Annoyed with herself, Vicki shook her head. Set a trap for her? Dad didn't do things like that. Time to go. She turned off the desk light and sneaked out into the hall, closing the door carefully behind her. She listened. Still no sound except the rhythmical murmur of the waves.

The hall and stairs ahead of her were brilliantly lit by the moonlight streaming in through the landing window. Of course, the moon was full. The mysterious powers that be had arranged that, too. Vicki shook her head again at such a silly idea. She made her way up to the attic.

A minute later she was standing beside the table with the Storm Goddess's head on it. She felt relieved that everything had gone so smoothly, but a little surprised as well. Not a single floorboard had creaked, although a lot of them had creaked quite loudly during her test run that evening. As for the lock on the attic door, which she'd definitely expected to squeak, it had opened as if it had just been oiled.

It was so light in the attic, she could have read a book. She went over to the window. From there she could look over the quay and out to sea. The bay lay glittering in the moonlight, almost entirely filled by the rising tide, and silvery waves were breaking far up the beach.

Vicki tiptoed over to the table. Silently, she pulled up one of the chairs and sat down in front of the Storm Goddess. Her eyes were now on a level with the head, but it was lying on its side. She tilted her own head until the Storm Goddess was looking straight at her. It suddenly seemed to Vicki, as a moonbeam slanted across the eyes, that they were alive, that the eyeballs had moved – that the Storm Goddess could really see! Hastily, she turned on the torch.

She took a deep breath, then adjusted the position of the head so that she could illuminate the hole in the neck. Bending forward, she peered into the cavity.

There they were, those lines and splotches on the side facing the eyes. Vicki could now see, in the beam of the torch, that they ranged in shade from grey to black. They looked almost like . . . like a photograph! That was it – like a black-and-white photograph imprinted on the wood. But how had they got there, and what were they meant to represent? Vicki peered through the opening in the neck. The lines and splotches did not form a picture. They looked like a photograph, but not a picture of anything in particular, just a black-and-grey jumble.

And then, in the midst of the silence, Vicki heard something creak. She jumped, listening hard. Nothing to be heard, just the murmur of the waves. The familiar, reassuring murmur of waves breaking on the beach. Vicki looked at the head. Could the timber have expanded in the warmth of the torch? Hey . . . what was that? The Storm Goddess's right eye was glowing . . . of course! Light was shining through the glass where the paint had flaked off. Just a moment . . . what shone in one direction could also . . .

She put the torch in the neck and carefully swivelled the head so that the opening was facing away from her. Her eyes were once more at the same level as those of the head. She tilted her own head so that the Storm Goddess was looking straight at her. That was the place where the light emerged. She put her eye to the Storm Goddess's eye and looked through it, and there, imprinted on the wood, there *was* a photograph.

But it still wasn't a *picture* of anything.

Vicki sat back. Why should it be a picture? It was probably just a black-and-grey muddle. Leaning forward again, she peered into the head. It was like looking through a magnifying glass . . . wait! Vicki sat quite still. Something had just occurred to her . . .

Gran's magnifying glass.

Vicki had experimented with it.

And she'd discovered something: not only could you look through it, you could shine a light through it – Gran's reading light, for instance. And if you held the glass right, an image of the reading light was projected on to the table-cloth. But . . . *the picture was upside down.*

The picture inside the Storm Goddess's head might be upside down, too.

If it *was* a picture.

Vicki leaned over sideways again, but the other way

around. The Storm Goddess was now looking at her the wrong way up, so to speak. Vicki peered through the eye . . .

There it was.

A picture.

It showed sails – the sails of a square-rigged ship. The rigging of the *Storm Goddess* must have looked like that. The picture was a view of the sails from somewhere aft, from the stern . . .

Vicki lifted her head.

A photograph taken from the stern?

That was crazy. It was *impossible* – figureheads were mounted on the prow.

She looked through the eye again. The lower sails were set, and the upper sails reefed as if a storm was brewing. And there was something hanging from the main yardarm – something that wasn't part of the rigging. Vicki stared at it, and at once realized what it was.

Suspended from the yardarm was a man.

A hanged man.

At that moment, silence fell.

At first she didn't understand what had happened. What was missing? What sound had suddenly ceased?

The waves. The sound of the waves was missing.

Vicki reached the window in two strides.

The bay lay there in the brilliant light of the full moon.
It was empty.
The bay was completely dry.
The sea had disappeared.

FOUR

It was nearly midnight, when the tide should have been at its highest, and the bay was brilliantly lit by the full moon. Vicki was standing on the sand below the quay. At high tide the waves would have been way over her head.

If there'd been any waves.

But there weren't. The bay was really and truly empty.

Not only near her but farther away and all along the beach, people accustomed since childhood to the rhythmical rise and fall of the tides were lining the shore. The sudden silence had woken them. Scarcely able to believe their eyes, they were staring out across the empty bay. None of them ventured out on to the mud flats, where the water should have been many feet deep.

In spite of this, Inspector Grogan and his sidekick,

Sergeant Willis, were driving up and down the beach in their police car. 'This is a police announcement!' Grogan bellowed through his megaphone. 'Don't go out on the mud flats! It's high tide. The water could come in at any moment!'

Vicki doubted it. She *knew* the tide wouldn't come in. Not yet, anyway. The sea had disappeared just as she had spotted the man hanging from the yardarm. It couldn't have been a coincidence. Coincidences like that simply didn't happen. On the other hand, the sea couldn't just disappear. It was puzzling, but the longer she thought about it, the more convinced she became that her discovery and the sea's disappearance were connected in some way. That was why the sea wouldn't reappear just like that. Something else would have to happen first, but what? The Storm Goddess, the hanged man, the sea's disappearance – if they *were* connected, *how* were they connected?

The Storm Goddess had yielded up her secret, but now it seemed to be only a part of a much bigger secret. A gigantic secret.

She *had* to find Peter.

He must be on the beach, but the beach was miles long and thronged with people, and it wasn't easy to see clearly even in the bright moonlight.

Vicki had run first to a spot on the quay near the town

hall because that was where she expected the action to be. But the harbour master hadn't put in an appearance, curiously enough.

Last February, when a violent storm had threatened to breach the sea defences near the harbour, he'd turned up at once and 'personally supervised emergency measures,' as the *Bay Gazette* had reported the next day. However, a subsequent article, signed 'Rose Redd', said that those same sea defences had been neglected by the local authorities – in other words, by the harbour master himself. Vicki's father read it with a smug smile at the breakfast table. Rose Redd had just joined the paper. She didn't come from the area, and Vicki wondered if that was even her real name.

After touring some more remote stretches of beach in their police car, Grogan and Willis returned. Sergeant Willis, who was at the wheel, pulled up right beside the quay and they both got out. Grogan heaved himself out of his seat, breathing heavily. He was pretty fat for a policeman, whereas Sergeant Willis was thin and wiry, with a peaked cap perched on his sticking-out ears. They climbed up the steps on to the quay and took up their position on the top. Vicki followed them and hung around nearby.

The harbour master appeared at last. He emerged from the town hall and came striding along the pavement. He was a giant of a man – at least a head taller than most of the big men in town. 'That's why he keeps getting re-elected,' Vicki's father had told her. 'People think a chap that big can handle anyone and anything.'

'Everything under control, sir,' Inspector Grogan reported. 'I've warned them all to stand clear.'

The harbour master nodded. He was wearing a safari jacket with patch pockets. It's as if he's trying to show he's a match for anything, including the sea, thought Vicki. Except that there isn't any sea in sight.

'Anything else we can do?' asked Grogan.

'Do? Do? What are we supposed to do when the bay runs dry? That's just it: there's nothing we can do, not a thing.' The harbour master ran his eyes over the crowd that lined the shore. His face had darkened. 'All the same, we'd better do *something*. All right, Inspector, issue a flood warning.'

'A flood warning?' Grogan stared at him in disbelief. 'What for? I mean, what's the point?'

'Harbour master!' Rose Redd was advancing along the pavement brandishing her reporter's notebook.

'Oh no, not her! That's all I need.' The harbour master's face darkened still further. 'Did you hear what I said, Inspector?'

'Yes, sir!' Grogan and Willis hurried back to their police car, Grogan talking feverishly into his radio.

'Just a couple of questions, sir.' Rose Redd was a slim young woman with auburn hair that looked dark red in the moonlight. She produced a pen. 'Have you found out what caused this? The sea's disappearance, I mean?'

'Good evening, Miss Redd – or should I say good morning?' The harbour master gave her a broad smile. 'Well, I've been making some enquiries. That's why I couldn't come right away.'

'And?' Rose Redd held her pen poised. 'What have you found out?'

'Several things.' The harbour master counted them off on his fingers. 'In the first place, our neighbours further along the coast report that the sea is still there. Secondly, only our own bay has run dry. Thirdly, Miss Redd, there's no question of the sea having disappeared. Fourthly, this appears to be a local quirk of the tide. And fifthly, I've taken certain precautions.'

'In other words,' said the reporter, 'you've no idea why the sea has disappeared. What precautions have you taken?'

Just then the siren mounted on the roof of the town hall started to wail. The sound, which quickly increased in volume, became so piercing that Vicki stuck her fingers in her ears.

The sightseers on the beach stared up at the town hall in alarm. Was the siren on because the sea had disappeared, or had something else happened? The siren continued to wail. The harbour master, too, had plugged his ears.

But not Rose Redd. She was writing in her notebook – writing nonstop.

The town hall siren eventually stopped wailing, and another two sirens took over. Moments later a fire engine came wailing along the coast road, blue lights flashing, followed by a truck containing more equipment. The two vehicles pulled up just short of the spot where Rose and the harbour master were standing on the quay. The sirens fell silent, but the lights went on flashing. Doors were flung open, and firemen jumped out and proceeded to unroll their hoses. The men in the equipment truck started unloading sandbags.

Rose continued to scribble away.

The chief fire officer came hurrying along the quay. Once he reached the reporter he came to a halt and surveyed the empty bay in silence. He was a middle-aged man with a massive moustache which began to twitch up and down, more and more violently, then came to rest. Without looking at the harbour master, he said, 'We were called out, so we came – we always do. We come when there's a fire. We come when there's flooding – when there's *too much* water.' His voice rose to a shout. 'But not when there's *no* water at all!' He turned to the other man.

'What's going on, harbour master? You want us to hose down the mud flats or something? Get it all back on board, boys!' he called to his crew, and stomped off down the slope.

Rose went on writing.

The harbour master's face had turned crimson. He flung out his chest and yelled, 'Inspector! Come here!'

Grogan came panting up the steps to the quay. 'What is it, sir?'

'Why on earth did you issue that alert, hmm?'

'But, but . . . ' Grogan stammered. 'It was you that—'

'I was talking about *future* precautions, man, that's all.' The harbour master turned to Rose Redd. 'The drying-up of the bay could be an ecological alarm signal, that's why. There's obviously been some misunderstanding. Oh well,' he said with a smile, 'these things can happen in the heat of the moment.' He turned to Grogan, who was staring at him open-mouthed. 'For now, leave it at the measures we discussed. Warn everyone to keep out of the tidal basin. Don't let them put themselves at risk.' He turned back to Rose. 'Any more questions, or is everything clear?'

Rose had stopped writing. 'Not absolutely everything.'

Vicki came downstairs in the morning to find her father and Eileen already having breakfast at table seventeen, the one the family used until the restaurant opened for lunch. Her father nodded to her and buried himself in his paper again. Vicki's only response to Eileen's 'Morning, sleep well?' was a grunt that might at a pinch have passed for 'Yes.' She was tired, dog tired.

The night before, she had felt very lonely when Rose Redd hurried off to her newspaper office, when the harbour master realized that he wasn't earning any brownie points and disappeared too, when Inspector Grogan and Sergeant Willis also drove off, when the excitement subsided a little and the sightseers on the beach realized that the sea had really, truly gone. She'd stood there on the sea wall, all alone with her secret.

The secret of the Storm Goddess.

And though it was late, she still felt that she had to find Peter, so she'd set off hoping to track him down.

But she'd had no luck.

And now too little sleep. Far too little.

'The channel is dry as a bone,' her father reported from behind his newspaper. 'And the harbour. All the boats are aground.'

Eileen looked surprised. 'Is it in the paper already?'

'They printed a special supplement.' It was just a single sheet, half the size of the newspaper but printed on both sides. 'They must have been at it all night, especially that

Redd woman. Most of this stuff is by her.' He read aloud: '"Thanks to the flood warning in the middle of the night, our community was thrown into a panic for no good reason. Just who issued the flood warning is unclear. However, the harbour master cannot escape criticism for failing to issue clear instructions in a situation that called for strong leadership."' Dad nodded with grim satisfaction.

'Does it say *why* the sea has disappeared?' Eileen asked.

He shook his head. 'The experts are baffled. What's really puzzling is the entrance to the bay. They showed it on the early morning news. There's water outside the entrance but none inside it.'

'Still,' said Eileen, 'the sea must start somewhere.'

'Yes, but the bottom of the bay is below sea level, so the water should flow in through the entrance, but it doesn't. It simply sloshes to and fro as if it keeps coming up against an invisible obstacle. Very mysterious.'

Vicki, who knew the Storm Goddess's secret, sat there eating her cereal and looking unconcerned. She got up. 'I think I'll go for a walk.'

Her father nodded. 'OK, but could you help out at lunchtime? We're bound to be busy. Without any sea, the tourists won't know what else to do.'

'Of course,' said Vicki.

In the meantime, she'd decided not to bank on Peter just

showing up. Instead, she'd find him. She would head for the left-hand side of the bay and try each hotel in turn.

Should she take her bike? No. Cycling along that stretch was prohibited, and the coast road behind it was out of sight of the mud flats, which was where Peter might be exploring.

She started walking along the quay. The bay stretched away on her right. It was a sight that jolted her awake in a flash. Last night the empty expanse had looked unreal and mysterious; the moon's silvery light had, in a way, made up for the lack of water. Now, in daylight, the flat, dry basin with its encircling quay looked about as appealing as a crater on the moon.

But at least it wasn't a *deserted* crater. As usual at this time, when the tide would normally have been out, the mud flats were dotted with people, most of them families with young children. Many were standing where the water's edge had been only yesterday, scanning the horizon for a glimpse of the sea.

Vicki squinted and followed their gaze. Wasn't that water shimmering in the distance? No, it was her imagination. The neck of the bay was slightly skewed, so the open sea wasn't visible from here.

A party of tourists had gathered around Captain Ahab and his band in front of the town hall. Old Ahab raised his arm and pointed in the direction of the mud flats, the band struck up 'Anchors Aweigh', and they all trooped off.

Walking on, Vicki soon reached the lifeboat station, beyond which lay Phil's trailer. She paused to look. There were people standing at every table and jostling for places at the counter. Vicki had trouble getting through. 'Hi, Phil,' she said. 'Looks like you're the in place now.'

'Yeah, I'm in because the sea's out.'

Vicki laughed.

'Like some chips?' Phil asked. 'They're nice and fresh.'

She shook her head. 'No thanks, just had breakfast.' She checked out the people at the tables.

'Round the corner,' said Phil.

'Huh?'

'Little round glasses with black frames?'

She nodded mutely.

'Take a look round the back.'

FIVE

Sure enough, there he was.

There was a lone table behind the trailer, and standing at it was Peter.

On the table were a can of Coke and a bag of chips, and beside them lay his telescope. His good old, not-so-stupid telescope.

Vicki grinned.

Just then he looked up.

She hurriedly wiped the grin off her face.

Peter smiled at her. 'Hi, Vicki,' he said.

Vicki smiled back at him. 'I was beginning to think your parents had whisked you off to the Costa del Sol.' He looked at her enquiringly, so she said, 'I've been looking for you.'

'You have?'

'Something's happened,' she blurted out. 'Something I wanted to tell you about.'

'Really?' He looked at her expectantly.

'I've discovered the Storm Goddess's secret!'

It was funny. Vicki had always thought that explaining and describing things wasn't her strong point, but she gave Peter a full and clear account of all that had happened. She felt genuinely proud of herself.

There was only one problem: Peter didn't believe her. 'That would be amazing,' he said. 'Except that it's impossible.'

'You think I'd make it up, a thing like that?'

'Er, no, of course not, but . . . an eighteenth-century photograph of a hanged man inside a figurehead? I mean, it does sound a bit unlikely.'

'The picture's there, you can have a look yourself. Besides, just look out across the bay. What you see is *totally* unlikely, but it happened.'

'That's true.' Peter thought for a moment. 'Why are you so sure that finding the picture and the sea's disappearance are connected?'

'Because they happened at the same time.'

'That could just be a coincidence.'

Vicki could only shrug.

Peter was still thinking. 'I read somewhere,' he said, 'that if you can explain one part of something, the whole thing becomes far more believable.'

Vicki thought that sounded logical. But why should something need explaining before he could believe it? It had happened, wasn't that enough? However, Vicki told herself, perhaps your mind has to work like Peter's if you want to become a scientist.

'Know what?' he said. 'We *do* have something we may be able to explain.'

Now it was her turn to look expectant.

'I have an idea – I mean, about how the photo ended up in the Storm Goddess's head. The restorer said something about a solution of mercury, didn't he?'

'Yes.'

'Hmm,' said Peter. 'That could have something to do with it. It *could* have, but I have to find out for sure.' He looked up at her. 'Hey, you know something? This is turning out to be a pretty cool holiday.'

Because he has a scientific problem to solve, or because he's met me? wondered Vicki.

He looked at his watch. 'I've got to go,' he said.

Oh well, thought Vicki, solving problems obviously means more to a scientist than anything else.

'My parents were still asleep when I left. They'll get mad if they wake up and find I'm not there. They might even decide to fly to Spain for the rest of their holiday.'

'But I thought it was their birthday present to you, staying at the seaside.'

'True, but there isn't any sea.' Peter looked at her. 'It'd be a real pain if I had to go.'

Vicki looked away quickly.

'OK,' he said. 'See you at the restaurant at lunchtime?'

'Bother, I forgot. I have to work at lunchtime.'

'That doesn't matter, does it?'

'Not really.' Vicki smiled. Then something occurred to her. 'Hey,' she said, 'you're not leaving here till you've told me your last name and the name of your hotel, and your mobile phone number.'

Peter jotted down the details on the paper napkin, and Vicki managed to pocket it without giving it a delighted glance first. 'Keep my table free for me, OK?' he said as he walked off.

With a pensive expression, Vicki watched him go. Then she picked up the empty Coke can and half-eaten bag of chips he'd left behind and took them to the litter bin at the front of the trailer. As she turned the corner she caught sight of a slim young woman with auburn hair standing at the counter.

Rose Redd was writing in her notebook. Naturally, what else would she be doing?

Except . . . what was there to write about here? That Phil's business had picked up overnight? That wasn't exactly newsworthy.

At that moment, the reporter stopped writing. She put the notebook in her shoulder bag and gave Vicki a brief glance. A casual glance, so it seemed.

Or so it was *meant* to seem.

But it wasn't a casual glance at all.

Just as Rose Redd walked briskly off along the coast road, Vicki grasped the truth.

The reporter had been eavesdropping.

Standing at the counter, just around the corner, Rose had heard everything. She'd caught every word that had passed between Vicki and Peter.

She'd overheard Vicki's story.

Rose Redd knew that the ocean had disappeared because Vicki had discovered the photo of the hanged man.

Keeping customers away from table nineteen was about as easy as shooing wasps away from a jam jar.

It might have been a Sunday, the Seashell Restaurant was so crowded, and every table was occupied. Hordes of families with little children had arranged to meet there as a matter of course, and it seemed that the secret telephone network extended to the neighbouring resorts as well.

Vicki had asked Frank, the waiter whose tables included number nineteen today, to keep it free, but he'd merely shrugged and hurried off.

She *needed* to speak with Peter as soon as possible, but she could hardly sit him down by the serving counter. She sighed.

Several things had happened since she and Peter had parted. For a start, she'd discovered that Rose Redd had been eavesdropping. Then, just as she was heading for the restaurant entrance after walking home along the quay, the reporter emerged. Vicki dodged behind a parked car, and Rose walked past without spotting her. No doubt about it: Rose Redd was snooping around after her.

Next, she'd found a TV crew in the restaurant.

Could Rose Redd be in cahoots with them?

No, she wasn't. The TV people were simply waiting for the sun to reach the portrait of the ship's captain on the wall. They needed some film footage. 'We're supposed to be doing a piece on the sea's disappearance,' the director had told Vicki's father, 'but how can you film something that isn't there any more?' So the ship's captain and the restaurant's seashell-lined walls were scheduled to appear on TV instead. A shame the Storm Goddess was up in the attic.

Except that she wasn't. When the TV crew had gone, Vicki's father told her – in the casual tone he always adopted when the Storm Goddess was involved – that Mr Pacino had taken the head away.

Why so soon? Now she wouldn't be able to show the picture to Peter! Perhaps his doubts about her story would persist, even if he'd since discovered how the photo inside the head might have got there.

Frank was clearing away table nineteen just as Peter appeared. A couple headed for the table, but Vicki – at a nod from Eileen – forestalled them by plunking a reserved sign down on it.

When Vicki and Peter were finally together, they both said, 'I've got something to tell you!' at the same time, which made them burst out laughing. Looking at Peter, Vicki realized that she'd seen him smile and chuckle, but she'd never heard him laugh before, not really. It was a nice laugh, and she hoped it wouldn't be the last time she heard it.

'What about your parents? Have they booked a flight to Spain?'

Peter shook his head. 'No way. Before we got here they were scared I might expect them to plod along the beach with their jeans rolled up and backpacks on, but that's out now that the sea's gone. They're perfectly happy lying on their deckchairs beside the pool.' He smiled at her. 'Well, who's going to start?' he asked, sitting down at table nineteen. He really wasn't the kind of boy to stand on ceremony.

'You'd better go first,' said Vicki, who was hoping he'd found out how the photo in the Storm Goddess's head had originated.

'Right,' he said. 'I've been rooting around in your public library. Did you know it has an encyclopedia dated 1830?'

Vicki shook her head. Typical of the local library to be so out of date. An encyclopedia dated 1830 . . . as if *that* could tell you all you needed to know about photography!

'I looked up an article on mercury,' Peter went on. He drew a deep breath, clearly about to launch into a long explanation. 'And—'

'Miss?'

Vicki had to hurry off.

Several minutes later, when she finally came back for a rest, Peter said, 'I'd better make it quick before you're called away again.' And he swiftly told her what he'd found in the old encyclopedia: that salts of mercury or mercuric oxide had been used for preserving timber, not only around 1830 but also earlier, during the eighteenth century; that under certain conditions, mercuric oxide turned black when exposed to light, but only if sufficient oxygen was present; and that the black discoloration could be fixed with a solution of salt. 'With sea water, for instance,' said Peter. 'In short, there *is* a way in which the photo could have appeared.'

'You mean you believe it exists?' Vicki asked. Peter nodded, so she went on: 'That's good, because I can't show it to you now.' And she told him why.

He wasn't as disappointed as she'd feared. 'Never mind,' he said. 'At least one of us has seen it – that's good enough.' He thought for a moment. 'But if the picture was taken from the rear of the boat, why would the head have been removed and transferred there?'

'It's called the stern.'

Peter laughed. 'Aye-aye, Skipper.' He looked over at the portrait on the wall. 'And who was the hanged man? Why was he hanged? Was he executed on the captain's orders?'

'It could have been the crew,' said Vicki. 'Without any orders. Perhaps there was a mutiny.'

'Could be,' Peter said, nodding. 'So the question remains: what happened on board the *Storm Goddess*?' He was still staring at the captain. 'I did a bit more rooting around in the library. I thought there might be some reference to the *Storm Goddess* before she went down.'

'Well?' Vicki said. 'Did you find anything?'

He shook his head. 'Nothing. Just the old town records, which contain a report of the storm in the autumn of 1772.'

'Yes,' said Vicki. 'I've read that too. Local history. We did it at school.'

'The packet that was washed ashore with the head – does anyone know what was in it?'

'No. At least, I've asked, and nobody seems to know what became of it.'

Peter adjusted his glasses. 'Somebody made it waterproof. What would have been valuable enough to protect in that way?'

'Waitress! Bill, please.'

'Coming.' Vicki stared into space. Then she said slowly, 'Writing. Something written in ink.'

'The bill!'

Vicki hurried off again.

When she came back, Peter said, 'Writing? On a sailing ship in those days? Something so valuable, it had to be preserved?'

'It could have been the ship's log,' said Vicki. 'The book in which the captain recorded everything that happened on board. Maybe he chucked it over the side at the last moment so it would be found. Like a shipwrecked sailor's message in a bottle.'

'If only we could find out where it is now,' said Peter.

'That would be something!' Vicki said.

Then she remembered Rose Redd.

'Someone overheard us this morning,' she said quickly, and she told him who it was and how she'd seen Rose coming out of the restaurant. 'What if she writes something about it in the paper?'

Peter frowned. 'We'd be in big trouble, that's for sure. I can just imagine that fat cop putting us through the wringer.' He paused. 'Still, she doesn't have any proof.'

'Yes, she does,' said Vicki. 'All she has to do is go to the restorer and get him to show her the head.'

They both lapsed into a gloomy silence.

Why did Rose Redd have to poke her nose in? The Storm Goddess's secret was no business of hers. Vicki looked up at the place on the wall from which the head had gazed down so recently. 'We need to find that log book.'

Vicki's grandmother lived in one of the cottages overlooking the harbour. Her husband, the father of Vicki's father, had been a sea captain. His name was on a headstone in the graveyard, but he wasn't buried there. He'd been 'lost at sea', as the headstone phrased it. Or, as Gran put it with brutal simplicity, 'drowned'. Vicki's father had been about her age when Grandpa's ship had gone down.

It was eight o'clock that night when Vicki rang the doorbell. Her grandmother answered it at once. A tall, scrawny woman, she was swathed in the pink kimono Grandpa had brought her from Japan long ago. 'Come in quick, our nonexistent ocean is on TV.'

The TV reporter was standing on the sea wall, holding a microphone under the harbour master's nose. 'The ecological impact could be really serious,' the harbour master was saying. 'We're particularly concerned about the shellfish population of the mud flats.'

'Pompous idiot!' Gran growled.

'What is more,' the harbour master went on, 'the financial damage should not be underestimated. Our town is a seaside resort, so the sea is the basis of our local economy. No sea, no tourists, no business.'

'Well, he's right there,' said Gran, 'too right.'

The report cut to a shot of a family loading some luggage into their car. 'The first holidaymakers are already leaving,' said the voice-over, 'and it's the height of the season.'

Vicki realized that the sea's disappearance was already causing considerable problems, and that she herself might be to blame. She wasn't, of course, but she couldn't help feeling a little bit responsible.

The next shot was of the Seashell Restaurant. The camera lingered on the captain's portrait, then panned across the shells lining the walls. Meanwhile, the voice-over continued: 'Local restaurants such as the Seashell Restaurant, a special favourite with families, will not be able to survive without the tourist business. The beaches will be deserted unless the sea returns. Its disappearance is still a total mystery. Now back to the studio.'

Gran turned off the TV. 'Not a bad advertisement for your daddy's restaurant,' she said, 'but I wonder why they didn't show the Storm Goddess.'

Vicki told her why.

'Well,' said Gran, 'fortunately, the harbour master will have to foot the restorer's bill. The head belongs to him. Poor man, that's his bad luck.' She made such an exaggeratedly mournful face that Vicki couldn't help but laugh. 'No, seriously,' she went on, 'a job like that can be expensive. But the head was inherited by the captain's descendants, and they include him.' She gave Vicki a nod. 'We're better off in that respect, eh?'

'We are? Why?'

'Because we only inherited the packet.'

Vicki looked puzzled. 'What packet?'

'The one that was washed ashore with the head, of course.'

SIX

Vicki stared at her grandmother. 'You mean *our family* inherited the packet? The one that was found at the same time as the head?'

'Yes, of course. But . . . ' Now it was Gran's turn to stare. 'You mean you didn't know?'

'No!' Vicki exclaimed. 'I didn't!'

'Good heavens!' said Gran. 'You didn't know that the packet contained a journal? The journal was destroyed in a fire, but luckily it had already been printed in book form beforehand. The book is a family heirloom now, handed down through the generations. You really didn't know about it?'

'No, Gran! No, I didn't!' Vicki clasped her hands together. 'Please tell me about it – *all* about it!'

'Hmm,' Gran said. 'You'll inherit the book someday, and your father has never mentioned it to you?'

Vicki shook her head.

'Strange,' muttered Gran.

'Please tell me about the book!' Vicki entreated. 'Where is it?'

'I don't know.'

'You *don't?*'

'I gave it to your father quite some time ago. No idea where he keeps it, though I can guess.' Gran looked at Vicki thoughtfully. 'Maybe I'd better leave it to him to tell you about the book.'

'No, Gran, *you* tell me! Please!'

But the old woman had made up her mind. She shook her head firmly. 'No, I can't. Your father will tell you when he thinks the time is right.'

Vicki felt almost sick with disappointment.

'Still, who knows?' said Gran. 'Maybe you'll come across the book before then.' She gave Vicki a meaningful stare. 'Purely by chance, of course.'

Vicki set off for home around half past nine. She couldn't wait a moment longer.

The log book of the *Storm Goddess*!

And she knew where it was.

Well, to be more accurate, she had a good idea where to look and she felt sure she'd find it. Why? Because today was her lucky day. One fortunate coincidence had helped her to meet up with Peter. Another had enabled her to keep table nineteen free for him. And another had put her on the track of the *Storm Goddess*'s log book.

Of course she would have to postpone her search until everyone in the building was asleep. The restaurant stayed open until after midnight, so that could be late. Very late. Should she risk it any earlier? It would soon be completely dark.

A wind had sprung up, and the sky had clouded over. Was a thunderstorm brewing? That would be unusual for this time of year. She regretted not riding her bicycle to Gran's. She was walking along the coast road but would retreat to the nearby hedge at the first sign of lightning.

It wasn't entirely dark yet, so she could still see the bay. Not all of it, but roughly as far as the tide came up to at this hour – or would have come up to if there'd been any. As she made her way along the road in the semi-darkness, she thought she saw shadowy figures moving around in the bay. It was only her imagination, of course, but she walked even faster, especially as the wind was strengthening.

A gale was blowing by the time she reached home, but it seemed that the storm couldn't decide whether to break or not. She paused in the entrance to the restaurant. Over half the tables were occupied, and Mike and Frank, the two waiters, were serving dinner. That meant the kitchen was still busy and her father preoccupied.

Could she risk it?

Frank and Mike hadn't seen her yet, nor had Eileen at the counter. Vicki slowly sidled out again and closed the door with care, then went round to the back entrance. The door served as a fire exit, so it couldn't be shut while customers were in the restaurant. The kitchen door along the hallway was always left open to stop anyone sneaking in unobserved, but Vicki felt sure she could slink past without being spotted by her father or one of his kitchen staff. Today was her lucky day, after all.

'Hello, back already?' Her luck didn't seem to work with Dad, but then, what was it he always said? 'A good chef needs eyes in the back of his head' – and he was a good chef.

'Yes,' said Vicki, 'I felt like an early night.' She peered through the doorway at the board with the orders pinned to it. Five meals to go. Dad might show up anywhere after that. It would be tricky . . .

He nodded. 'Fine, have a good long sleep.' Something started sizzling on one of the burners. 'Don't let that oil get too hot!' he barked over his shoulder. 'How many times do

I have to tell you!' Then, amiably, to Vicki: 'OK, good night.'

'Good night, Dad.' She ran upstairs to the attic and hurriedly unlocked the door.

Bother, she'd forgotten her torch. Should she go back for it? No. Should she risk turning the light on? Although it was only a naked bulb hanging from a beam, anyone outside the building would be able to tell that someone was up in the attic. On the other hand, she would be able to see better. She flicked the switch.

There was the unused table, its surface now bare, with the rickety chairs around it.

And there was the old trunk. It looked enormous – far bigger than it had ever looked before. Finding the book could take her some time. She grasped the handles on the lid, drew a deep breath – the lid was heavy – and threw it back.

Vicki had known that the trunk wasn't locked; she'd rummaged through its contents once before – at least, she'd started to do so, because she'd soon given up. The trunk was chock-a-block with files full of boring things like old menus and household bills.

She heaved out one bundle of files after another, only to find more files beneath them. No, not files, folders. The bottom of the trunk was lined with faded blue, red and yellow folders. She removed one of them. There was something written in pencil on its flap. It was her father's name, and beneath it, his class in school: Lower Fourth.

She opened the folder.

And found herself looking at a sailing ship.

It was a drawing of an eighteenth-century square-rigged sailing ship, complete in every detail, including several sailors on deck. The heads of the figures were a bit out of proportion, but the rigging was correctly drawn.

The drawing was her father's work. He'd written his name and class in the bottom right-hand corner.

He'd also given the ship a regulation figurehead on her prow.

Vicki recognized it at once, because he'd made a pretty good job of the figure's head and had written the name of the ship on her bow: *Storm Goddess*.

Shaking her head in disbelief, Vicki quickly leafed through the rest of the drawings. One sailing ship after another, sometimes in harbour, sometimes out at sea, sometimes in a storm, sometimes becalmed, but always the *Storm Goddess*.

She stared into space.

So there'd been a time when her father was a fan of the *Storm Goddess*.

But he wasn't a fan of the *Storm Goddess* any more.

Why?

She peered into the trunk. One of the folders might hold the answer to the mystery, but how could she look through them all right now?

She cocked her head and listened. Normal restaurant noises. The gale was blowing even harder, but that was all.

No, the mystery of her father could wait. What mattered now was the mystery of the *Storm Goddess*.

But the ship's log might also be hidden in one of the folders, so she would have to look through them all anyway. She'd just started to do that when an idea struck her.

She picked up one folder after another to see if there was anything underneath, and the fourth time she hit the jackpot: two slim books, each with a pale-green paper cover.

She took out the first one and opened it: *A Herbalist's Handbook*. Shoot! She was about to sling it back into the trunk when she heard footsteps below.

Her father – he was climbing the stairs!

She listened intently. He had reached the second floor. She heard him walk along the hallway. Silence followed, broken only by the whistling of the wind. Presumably he'd paused outside his bedroom door.

Then, all at once, more footsteps. The attic stairs creaked. He was on his way up!

The light under the door . . . with one cat-like bound, Vicki reached the switch and turned it off.

She held her breath.

Her father had now reached the top of the stairs. Nearer and nearer he came, then halted.

He was right outside the door. What on earth could he be after? An old bill, an old recipe? Whatever it was, he *mustn't* come in.

Go away, thought Vicki. Go away! If she concentrated hard enough, she felt, the idea couldn't fail to take root in her father's head. Go away!

And then she heard his footsteps again. Back to the top of the attic stairs, down them and along the second-floor hallway, then down to the first floor.

Vicki drew several deep breaths. It had been a close-run thing, but luck *was* on her side after all. She turned the light on again.

Quick now. If her father had been looking for some old bills or something, it meant that he'd finished work in the kitchen. He often went for a stroll along the quay at closing time, so he would be bound to see the light in the attic window. However, the wind was getting steadily stronger and the storm seemed to have decided to break in earnest. He probably wouldn't venture outside, but she would have to hurry nonetheless.

She reached for the other little book, then hesitated. What if her father hadn't stashed the ship's log book in the trunk? No, this had to be where it was. In two seconds she would be reading the words 'Log Of The Good Ship *Storm Goddess*' or something of the kind, she felt sure.

All the same, she shut her eyes and opened the book by touch. Would her luck continue to hold? Now! She blinked once, blinked again – and opened her eyes wide. The title page read:

Journal kept by
the FIRST MATE
of the 'Storm Goddess'
ON HER FINAL JOURNEY

She shook her head.

It wasn't the ship's log at all.

But . . .

The first mate?

The one who was an ancestor of hers!

Her ancestor, the first mate, had kept a record of what had happened on board the *Storm Goddess*!

Vicki's sigh of delight was almost as loud as the wind blowing outside.

Although her father never would have entered her bedroom without knocking, she locked the door for safety's sake.

She had replaced the folder of drawings and the herbalism book in the trunk and tossed the files in on top of them – in the right order, of course. This made a bit of noise, but no one indoors could have heard it because the wind had developed into a full-blown storm. It whistled around the building and rattled the tiles on the roof in quite an alarming way.

Vicki pulled the blind down over the window, then sat at her desk and turned on the table light. If she heard her father coming upstairs she would turn it off in double-quick time. Finally, she opened the book.

There was more than one line on the title page – she'd already noticed that. Printed on yellowing, speckled paper, the introduction read as follows:

Journal kept by

the FIRST MATE

of the 'Storm Goddess'

ON HER FINAL JOURNEY

The tale of that ill-starred vessel which, during the great tempest that raged in the autumn of the Year of Our Lord 1772, was engulfed by the waves together with all her crew when approaching her port of origin, all that remained of her being the head of the wooden figure mounted on her bow and the aforesaid journal, which same was wrapped in sailcloth and rendered proof against the elements with pitch.

Vicki turned the page.

Foreword by the Publisher

The first mate's journal was wrapped in several layers of sail-cloth, all of which had been carefully sealed with pitch. However, the packet displayed an unaccountable rent, which had doubtless been inflicted just before it was committed to the waves. Although, as luck would have it, the innermost layer of sailcloth remained undamaged, some of the watery element so inimical to paper and ink had seeped through notwith-standing. In consequence, certain passages were regrettably obliterated. In the ensuing text, these passages are indicated thus: [Illegible].

Vicki continued to turn the pages.

We have now been at sea for more than eighty days . . .

She raised her head. The wind raging outside made it sound as if the bay was being lashed by a full-blown equinoctial storm. But no rain was lashing the window-panes, nor could she hear any thunder. She went over and raised the blind a few inches. No sign of lightning. A summer storm without lightning? Odd. Vicki sat down at the desk again. It *was* odd, a summer storm as violent as this. Really weird. She read on.

. . . *but the* Storm Goddess *will soon, after an eventful voyage, be dropping anchor in the safety of her home port. Or so*

I hope and pray.

It is the events of the last few hours that have prompted me to take up my pen at this juncture, when I trust that our voyage will soon be over. A cruel injustice has been done, but I, being the first mate of this vessel, must bear some responsibility for it. I write these words in the hope of unburdening my soul in some small measure.

But I am guilty nonetheless. We are all of us guilty, and I suspect that we shall have to pay a terrible price for our misdeeds.

Much has happened during this voyage, and much of it was iniquitous. It was desired and encouraged by the ill-disposed among us, the captain first and foremost. And the well disposed? At best, they held their peace, but oh, how many of them participated in word and deed!

For the gold was too great a temptation.

The captain has yet to tell us how much the sale of our prize yielded. I estimate the proceeds at approximately fifteen hundred gold doubloons. The captain has hidden the gold away, but I believe I am too well acquainted with his way of thinking not to be able to guess its whereabouts. Our voyage is nearing its end, however, and he will soon have to give each man his due share. Being the owner of the Storm Goddess as well as her master, he will naturally keep the biggest share for himself, but a vast sum in gold will remain for distribution to every ship's officer – myself included, it shames me to admit! The balance will be shared out among the crew according to rank. Even an able seaman, for example, will receive as much gold as will purchase the poor wretch a modest cottage and a plot of land.

That being so, even the well disposed among us have shut their eyes to the fact that this gold was ill-gotten.

The price to be paid for it is silence. Never must any of us divulge how he acquired his wealth. This was the very cause of today's occurrence, which has brought my spirits to their lowest ebb.

It all began when the weather turned so foul . . .

Wham! The window was lashed by a gust so violent that it threatened to blow in the panes. The gale was now howling and rampaging around the building like one of those autumn storms that make it advisable to close the shutters and bolt them. It was quite possible that Dad and Eileen had already started to do so. Vicki listened, but the raging storm drowned out every other sound. Should she take a look downstairs? No. She had to find out what had happened aboard the Storm Goddess.

. . . that the captain set half-reefed storm-sails for safety's sake. Sure enough, the sea became exceeding rough, but we were undismayed until it was reported from the fo'c'sle that the head of the figurehead had come adrift and was threatening to fall off into the sea. As every sailor knows, the loss of a figurehead, or of parts thereof, is an infallible sign of impending disaster.

The evil tidings were brought by a young sailor whose first voyage this was, and whom all on board had taken to calling 'Simple Simon'. If the truth be told, the poor lad was so simple and weak in the head that he might justly have been called an imbecile. But he was strong and willing and well liked by the crew, albeit they were forever playing cruel tricks on him – so much so that I, being a ship's officer, was more than once obliged to intervene for his protection.

On receiving this news, the captain bethought himself of a way to dispel any fears that might have arisen among the crew. He bade the ship's carpenter remove the head of the figurehead and lash it to the aftermast, where all could see it. The carpenter promptly did so, but in his haste he inadvertently chipped some paint off the right eye – an occurrence unworthy of mention had it not sent the captain into such a blind, insensate rage. It was evident that he, too, had succumbed to the nervous apprehension that now prevailed on board.

That the head had been taken to a place of safety did not appear to have reassured the men in any way. They cast furtive glances at the afterdeck and could be seen whispering together in small groups. The boatswain eventually reported that many of the crew regarded it as an evil omen that the head and body of the figurehead had never been a single piece of timber. No good could come of a voyage undertaken with such a figurehead, nor, in particular, of the gold acquired in course of that voyage. The gold had been ill-gotten, and many of them had a mind to inform the authorities of its provenance.

The captain acted without delay. The storm had unexpectedly abated. The sea was still rough, but the wind had dropped, so he ordered the entire crew to assemble amidships.

Addressing the men, he reminded them that their gold had indeed been acquired unlawfully, but that they had all, without exception, helped to obtain it. Moreover, if a single one of them broke his silence, they would not only forfeit their gold but render themselves liable to severe penalties. Indeed, they might even end on the gallows.

The captain then commanded each man to step forward and swear on the Bible and on his soul's salvation never to breathe a word about the manner in which he had obtained his gold.

And one man after the other stepped forward and swore the oath demanded of him. They did so without grumbling, indeed, with a will, for they had grasped that only thus, by preserving a steadfast silence, could they enjoy theirill-gotten gains.

The last in line was Simple Simon. He raised his right hand and seemed about to swear the oath without demur, like the rest, when all of a sudden he started to shed bitter tears. On being asked what ailed him, he replied:

'The parson told us: "Those with ill-gotten gains never prosper." And the schoolmaster told us: "Ill-gotten gains will burn your house down."' Before he could swear the oath, therefore, he would have to ask leave of the parson and the schoolmaster.

His words were followed by a deathly hush.

I doubt if any member of the crew had failed to comprehend what a threat the lad represented. They all knew that, even if he were prevailed upon to swear the oath, they could never rest assured that he would keep it.

The men became restive. They exchanged whispers with their neighbours and joined one or another of the groups that were forming everywhere. In short, they held a council of war.

Had circumstances been different, the captain would never have permitted the men to band together in such a way. As it was, he suffered them to do so because he knew what the result of their deliberations would be: a result that was wholly in keeping with his own wishes.

Before very long, the boatswain approached the captain. Speaking on the crew's behalf, he informed him that they had come to a decision. They had unanimously resolved to . . .

[Illegible]

Illegible, worse luck, and just at the crucial moment. Vicki read on.

How could things have come to such a pass? I must render an account of myself. I have time enough, for the wind has dropped entirely.

To think what a happy, contented man I was in the early summer of this year, when I was still serving as first mate on the Gertrude . . .

No, she certainly didn't want to read that now. She turned a few pages.

What could the crew's decision have been?

All at once, Vicki became aware of the storm raging outside the window. She genuinely hadn't noticed it while reading. The wind seemed to have strengthened still further – if possible. Any moment now, her father would knock on the door and ask if she wanted to come downstairs . . .

But what had the crew of the *Storm Goddess* decided?

She turned another page.

. . . *the events of the past few hours . . . a cruel injustice has been done . . .*

But of course! That was it!

The crew had decided to kill Simple Simon.

They had hanged him from the yardarm.

He was the dangling figure in the photograph inside the

Storm Goddess's head.

A sudden silence fell.

The storm had died.

Vicki could hear her own breathing in the stillness.

She jumped to her feet, dashed over to the window, and tugged at the blind. It shot up.

Brilliant moonlight. The sky was cloudless, and the moon as bright as it had been last night. Had the sea . . . ? No, all was quiet. No murmuring waves, nothing.

And then she had a premonition.

She hurried over to the chest of drawers beside her bed, pulled out the bottom drawer, the one she kept her odds and ends in, and rummaged around in it. There it was: her own telescope. Then she dashed out into the hallway, up the attic stairs, into the attic, and over to the window.

There lay the bay, brightly illuminated by the full moon.

It was still dry.

But something had changed.

In the middle of the bay, with her keel embedded deep in the mud and her masts jutting skyward, lay a sailing ship.

An ocean-going, eighteenth-century square-rigged sailing ship under full sail.

Vicki put the telescope to her eye and adjusted the focus

with trembling fingers.

There was the prow, complete with figurehead.

But the figurehead was headless.

And inscribed on the prow was the name: *Storm Goddess*.

SEVEN

The siren on the roof of the town hall had never scared the townsfolk.

But the storm had. It wasn't the raging wind that did it, it was the sudden hush.

Nearly everyone had woken up. And, because they'd all jumped to the conclusion that the sea was up to its tricks again, they streamed down to the beach. Without a second thought, most of them walked out over the mud flats to the sailing ship that lay high and dry in the middle of the moonlit bay.

Grogan and Willis made no immediate attempt to prevent the crowds from entering the tidal basin. They limited themselves to keeping them some distance from the ship. They succeeded in doing this only because the fire officers turned up promptly and cordoned off the area around the *Storm Goddess* with ropes strung between posts driven into the mud.

Vicki was standing in the midst of the crowd with her mountain bike.

She'd been the very first to reach the ship.

One glimpse of the *Storm Goddess* from the attic window had sent her tearing downstairs. She'd made a split-second decision to get her bike from the shed behind the restaurant – which was fortunate, since the ship was farther away than she'd thought.

That was how she'd got there before everyone else.

Absolute silence had reigned. Not a sound came from aboard the *Storm Goddess*.

Vicki's eyes hadn't deceived her: all the *Storm Goddess*'s sails were set, even the smallest of them, and many were in shreds.

No wonder, after that storm.

But which storm?

Tonight's storm, or the one that had sunk her two hundred and thirty years ago?

Either way, there she was.

The hull had embedded itself deep in the mud, ridges of which were piled up around her bow like waves thrust aside by a ship ploughing through rough seas – as if the *Storm Goddess* had flown into the bay and landed on the mud flats like an aeroplane. It was astonishing she hadn't come apart at the seams. But there she lay.

Firmly fixed in the mud, as if she could never be taken out to sea again.

Vicki walked along the side of the ship until she could see the backs of the sails attached to the mainmast. She looked up at the yardarm.

No one was hanging there.

What had happened between Simple Simon's execution and the sinking of the *Storm Goddess*?

Wait a minute . . . the ship couldn't have sunk. She was here in the bay, and she didn't look as if she'd been lying on the ocean floor for over two centuries. How come?

Vicki decided not to think about it.

Instead, she wondered what things looked like on deck. The body of the ship wasn't so far from the ground. It ought to be possible to climb aboard with the help of a fair-sized ladder.

She went back to the stern, rounded it, and walked along the port side.

And there, hanging from the bulwark amidships, was a rope ladder with wooden rungs.

It hung down to the ground.

Like a mute invitation.

While staring at the rope ladder, which gave her an easy way of reaching the deck of the *Storm Goddess*, Vicki suddenly felt she was being watched by someone on board. It was a vivid sensation, and it pierced her to the marrow.

She was still gazing up at the ship when Grogan's police car came roaring across the mud flats. Quickly, she ran to the bow, wheeled her bike behind the ridges of mud, and ducked down.

The harbour master, who was sitting in the passenger seat, jumped out even before the car came to a stop. He stood staring up at the *Storm Goddess* – at the headless figurehead and the name on the prow. 'My ancestor's ship,' he muttered. 'This is incredible.' He clasped his huge hands over his paunch and gazed in awe. 'It's like a miracle.'

But then he shook his head. 'Miracle or not,' he went on, squaring his shoulders and turning to Grogan, 'make sure nobody gets too close, OK?' More to himself than to the policeman, he added, 'I'm going to develop this into a tourist attraction. We may not have any sea, but at least we've got a ship.' He looked around. 'There are people coming. Move it, Inspector, head them off. And alert the fire department, but only over the radio. No sirens this time.'

Vicki had managed to take her bike and mingle with the crowd unnoticed by the harbour master or Grogan and Willis. They would have been bound to give her a hard time. In the first place, riding mountain bikes on the mud flats was strictly prohibited; secondly, explaining how she'd arrived so much more quickly than everyone else, even by bike, would have been a bit tricky.

'Well, how did you make *this* happen?'

Rose Redd had slunk up behind her. Vicki stiffened defensively. 'I've no idea what you mean.'

'Tell me another! I'd like to have a chat with you. Tomorrow sometime?'

Vicki shrugged. 'I really don't know what we'd have to talk about.'

The young woman eyed her intently. 'Well,' she said, 'think it over. I'll be in touch.' And she disappeared into the crowd.

Staring after her, Vicki felt her anger swelling. Why couldn't Rose Redd leave her alone? The secret of the *Storm Goddess* was hers, and this interfering busybody was completely spoiling it for her.

Just as she was thinking this, she caught another

glimpse, over the heads of the crowd, of the rope ladder hanging down the port side of the ship, and her anger evaporated.

Rose Redd didn't matter in the least.

It suddenly dawned on Vicki that only one thing mattered.

She *had* to get aboard the *Storm Goddess*.

It was nearly nine o'clock when Vicki woke up. It took her a moment to remember all that had happened. Then she jumped out of bed, grabbed her telescope, and ran upstairs to the attic in her pyjamas.

The bay was bathed in brilliant morning sunlight.

And in the middle – at the exact centre of the semi-circular basin, or so it seemed to Vicki – lay the *Storm Goddess*. She could make out the headless figurehead with her naked eye.

There were a lot of people milling around the ship, but only a few were really close to it. She put the telescope to her eye.

Although the fire department's rope barrier was still there, some workmen were busy erecting a chain-link fence inside it. It didn't look too hard to climb.

And the ladder was still hanging down the port side.

Vicki had thought of calling Peter last night, when she

was out there beside the ship, but he might have been asleep. Besides, his parents might have objected to him receiving phone calls after midnight, so she didn't.

But she could call him now. She went down to her bedroom and took out her mobile. 'Hi, Peter?'

'Hi, Vicki. I was just heading out to look at the *Storm Goddess*.' He hesitated for a moment. 'What did you do this time?'

That was more or less what Rose Redd had asked her. Why? Because she was after a story. Peter had asked the question because he was *in* the story, like Vicki herself. 'I'd rather explain in person. Meet you at the *Storm Goddess* in half an hour, OK?'

'OK.'

'On the port side,' she added. 'Where the rope ladder is.'

Vicki had just replaced the telescope in her drawer and was about to go downstairs when her mobile rang.

'Good morning, Vicki.'

'Oh, it's you, Gran. Hi.'

'Are you on your own?'

'Yes, I'm up in my room.'

'Good, then tell me something: Did you come across the book I mentioned?'

'Yes,' said Vicki. 'Last night. Purely by chance, of course.'

'Of course.' There was a brief silence. Gran went on, 'Look, Vicki, I've been thinking. You find the journal kept by the first mate of the *Storm Goddess*, and the *Storm Goddess* turns up in the bay the very same night. I mean, well . . . could the two things be connected in some way?' Quickly, she added, 'It's silly of me, I know, but . . . '

No, it wasn't silly of her at all, Vicki thought, but should she explain the connection now? Should she tell her the whole story, right from the beginning? That would take time, and what if Gran didn't believe her?'

'I don't understand,' she said. 'Connected how? What do you mean?'

'Nothing, nothing, I was only asking. Don't worry about it. See you soon, bye.'

Vicki went downstairs to the restaurant, where Dad and Eileen were still sitting having their breakfast. The *Bay Gazette* had printed another half-sheet supplement.

'Did the Redd woman write most of that, too?' asked Eileen.

'Yes,' said Dad. 'She seems to be a hard worker. She's obviously not scared of the harbour master, either. I like that.'

Eileen glanced at him quickly. 'Really?' she said. 'I think it's rather weird the way she always manages to be on the spot at the right time.'

Vicki could only nod in agreement. She buttered herself some toast without sitting down.

Her father read aloud: "'The harbour master emphasized that the owner of the *Storm Goddess* had been an ancestor of his, and that he therefore regards himself as the rightful owner. Now that the ship has suddenly reappeared, he plans to turn it into a tourist attraction. A government official from the Department of the Environment made only a brief statement on the subject last night. 'If the ship really is an eighteenth-century vessel,' he told our reporter over the phone, 'the identity of her original owner is quite irrelevant. The ship has now been taken over by the Society for Nautical Research and will naturally be off-limits to the general public. She will have to undergo thorough scientific examination. For the present, there is no question of using her as a tourist attraction – and, anyway,' said the official, who was clearly annoyed, 'that would require formal authorization.' So it would seem that the harbour master is not only planning to act on his own, in defiance of the authorities; he also claims that an item of government property – in other words, the property of the nation – belongs to him alone.'"

Vicki's father nodded with a look of satisfaction, as before.

'Well,' said Vicki, 'I'm off. I want to look at that ship.'

'All right, but listen: I've advertised for extra staff, but can you go on helping at lunchtimes till I find someone?'

'Of course,' said Vicki.

She made her way across the empty restaurant and out through the door. Shutting it behind her she turned – to find Rose Redd sitting on the steps. Her auburn hair gleamed in the sunlight. 'Hello, Vicki,' she said.

Vicki stiffened. 'The restaurant isn't open yet.'

Rose nodded. 'I know that, but I wanted to apologize for eavesdropping on you yesterday. OK?'

'It was just a joke, all that stuff I said,' Vicki began quickly. 'There isn't really any photo inside the head.'

'I could ask Mr Pacino to show it to me.'

True! What now? 'Go and ask him, then,' was all Vicki could think of to say.

'I already have.'

Vicki stared at her.

Rose sighed. 'Unfortunately, he'd already sprayed the hole in the head with preservative. The stuff's hardened, and there isn't a hope of removing it without destroying what's underneath.'

The photo was gone! Gone for ever!

Vicki would never see it again, but then, no one else would, either. All of a sudden it came to her: I'm the only one who saw that picture of the hanged man. It was *meant* for me.

She had told Peter the secret, and that was all right because he was in on this story like herself. But she had no intention of telling anyone else about it, ever.

'So you didn't see any photo inside the head?' asked Rose.

Vicki shook her head. 'There was nothing there. I made it all up.' And because grown-up turns of phrase worked best with grown-ups, she added, 'I was only trying to impress, the way people my age do.'

'Boys, yes,' Rose said and looked at her. 'Girls less so.'

Peter, as always, had his telescope with him. After Vicki had told him about the journal, he said, 'Come on, I've found something interesting to show you.'

She followed him along the chain-link fence to the starboard side of the ship.

The fenced-in area around the *Storm Goddess* was bigger than it had looked through her telescope from the attic window. Some earnest-looking men were pacing around inside the enclosure and conferring together in groups – presumably the scientists the Department of the Environment official had mentioned. Two television crews had also turned up. The harbour master was nowhere to be seen.

Peter led Vicki to a spot from which they could see the back of the sails on the mainmast. 'Look up at the main sail,' he said, handing her his telescope.

But Vicki had already seen it with her naked eye: hanging from the yardarm was a rope that clearly had no connection with the rigging or sails. It was simply hanging there with no purpose. With no purpose *now*, but it *had* had a purpose two centuries ago. It was the rope that had hanged Simple Simon.

Vicki took Peter's telescope and focused it at the end of the rope. It didn't look as if it had snapped, more like it had been severed.

'They must have cut him down,' said Peter. He stared up at the rope. 'Two hundred and thirty years ago.' He shook his head. 'And the ship looks as if it might have been built yesterday.'

Vicki handed back the telescope. 'Can you explain that?'

'No, because it can't have been, so I'm not even going to try.' He turned to face her. 'Why did you want us to meet by the rope ladder?'

'Have you looked at it?'

'Yes, it looks nice and strong. We could use it to climb on board. The fence shouldn't be too much of a problem.'

'Exactly.'

'But what would we do up there?'

'No idea.' Vicki looked at him. 'The sea disappeared and the ship appeared, and both things happened while I was on the trail of the Storm Goddess's secret.' She stared up at the rope dangling from the yardarm. 'You seriously think this ship is lying here for no good reason?' She turned to him again. 'Somebody's waiting for me to go aboard, I've no idea who or why. You see?'

'I see,' said Peter. He nodded. 'I'll come with you.' It sounded almost like a solemn vow. 'Tonight would be best. The only thing is . . . ' He frowned.

'What's the problem?'

'If my parents catch me sneaking off, I'll be in big trouble, and I can't tell them what we're doing.'

Vicki thought for a moment. 'We've got a guest room. I'm sure my dad and Eileen wouldn't mind if you slept over. D'you think your parents would let you?'

Peter looked dubious. Then he said, 'I'll manage it somehow.'

'Great, then I can show you the journal.'

Peter wanted to be back in time to have lunch at the hotel with his parents. Vicki walked some of the way with him. 'See you tonight,' he said when they were level with the fish and chip stand.

Watching him go, Vicki wondered why three simple

109

little words should set her insides dancing from the tips of her toes to the roots of her hair. And her outsides as well. She went skipping down to the trailer. 'Hi, Phil! Isn't it a wonderful day?'

'Depends who for.'

'I see what you mean.' Vicki looked around. Only one of Phil's tables was occupied. The postman, who always took a break here, was having coffee.

'Everyone's out at the ship,' said Phil, wiping his clean counter still cleaner with a sponge. 'But you know something? I've put in an application.'

'An application?'

'Yes, to the local authorities. I want to tow my trailer out to the ship and set it up there.'

Vicki shook her head. 'But, Phil, how will you do that?'

'You mean because there aren't any wheels on it?' Phil grinned. 'They're in the garage back home – I can jack this thing up and get it mobile anytime.' He turned serious. 'Oh, you mean because the mud flats are a protected area?' He shook his head. 'That doesn't matter any more, apparently.'

'So what *does*?'

'Dosh,' said Phil. 'Tourist money. In the long run, it's going to take a bit more than the sight of an old sailing ship to bring the holidaymakers flocking in. They'll be needing certain facilities – like my fish and chips, for instance.' Phil stopped wiping the counter. 'I bet you a pound to a penny the harbour master grants my application.'

Not for the first time, Vicki reflected that people who thought Phil was stupid were stupid themselves.

Vicki's lunchtime turned out to be quite relaxing. The decent wage Dad would pay her for three hours waiting tables would be easy money; the Seashell wasn't inundated with customers this time.

So she didn't mind when a man by himself sat down at table twelve, which was set for six diners.

Come to think of it, she couldn't recall ever seeing a man have lunch here by himself.

He had a shiny bald head, bushy eyebrows, and a nose like a potato.

She decided to wait till he'd looked through the menu, then wait a while longer before heading over to the table.

But the bald-headed man wasn't looking at the menu. He was surveying the restaurant. First he scanned the seashells on the walls, then he spent a considerable time staring at the base on which the Storm Goddess's head had hung, and finally he studied the captain's portrait. He seemed unable to tear his eyes away from it – indeed, he even swivelled his chair round for a better view.

Vicki went over to him. 'What can I get you?'

The bald-headed man's bloodshot little eyes regarded her from under his bushy eyebrows. His potato of a nose was stippled with blackheads. 'A glass of water, no ice.'

'A glass of water, no ice.' Vicki waited, but that was all he said. She indicated the menu. 'And, er, have you chosen?'

'No thanks, nothing to eat.'

'I see.' Occupying a table for six and ordering a glass of water? What a nerve!

Just as she turned to go, the bald-headed man said, 'You're the boss's daughter, aren't you?'

A chill ran down her spine. Of course, he must be a council inspector! She nodded.

'I'd like a word with you.'

She nodded again. 'OK, but I'll bring you your water first.' She hurried over to the counter. 'Eileen,' she whispered, 'I think that man at table twelve is from the council. He wants a word with me.'

Eileen gave him a quick glance. 'Never seen him before; he must be new to the job. Don't worry, though, he can't do anything to us. Keep your mouth shut, that's all.' Of course she would. She would never, even under hypnosis, have admitted that Dad was paying her.

'There you go.' Vicki put the glass down in front of him. He pointed to the chair across the table. She shook her head. 'I'd rather stand.'

'Suit yourself.' The bald-headed man said nothing for a moment. Then he asked abruptly, 'That carved wooden head – where's it gone?'

As if that was any of his business! Still, there was no need to make a secret of it. Vicki told him.

He regarded her again from under his bushy eyebrows, then rapped out his next question, 'A packet was washed ashore with that head in 1772. Your family inherited it, didn't they?'

That was *certainly* no concern of the council. 'I think you'd better speak to my father about it,' Vicki told him, and turned to go.

'Wait!' he said sharply. Vicki was so startled that she did as he asked. 'You wouldn't run away from the press, would you?'

So he wasn't from the council! 'You work for a newspaper?'

'Yes, the *Morning Post*. Belper's the name. I'm writing a feature on the *Storm Goddess*.'

The *Morning Post* served the big port farther along the coast. Vicki had heard her father mention that Rose Redd had worked for it before moving to the *Bay Gazette*. These reporters eager for a scoop wouldn't get anywhere with her.

The man named Belper said, 'I've already put a few facts together. That's how I found out that your family inherited that packet.' He paused, then added, 'Because it contained the journal of an ancestor of yours.'

EIGHT

Vicki stared at him speechlessly.

How did he know about the journal?

Just a minute . . .

They must have printed more than one copy, so perhaps he had managed to dig another one up somewhere.

But what did he want from her?

'I know your family had a printed copy of the journal.' Belper leaned forward and stared at her. 'I also know that the copy is now—'

'Vicki! Call for you!'

'In a minute,' Vicki called to Eileen.

'No, now! It's urgent!'

'I won't be long,' Vicki told Belper, and hurried over to the counter.

Eileen handed her the phone. 'It's your grandmother,' she said in a low voice. 'She sounds upset.'

'Vicki!' Gran really was in a state. 'Is that man Belper there?'

'Yes, but how do you—'

'He came to see me earlier. Pretended to be a reporter.'

'Pretended to be?'

'Yes. I had my doubts about him when he'd gone, so I called the *Morning Post*. They'd never heard of him.'

'You mean he *isn't* a reporter? But . . . in that case, who is he?'

'I don't know, Vicki, but listen. He knew we had the first mate's journal and asked if he could have a look at it.' Gran hesitated. 'I told him you had it and suggested he should ask you about it himself. It was stupid of me, I know, but he seemed so set on the idea – quite obsessed with it, in fact.'

'But if he isn't a reporter . . . I mean, what's he up to?'

'He's up to no good, I'm afraid, or he wouldn't have had to spin me that yarn. Just be careful, Vicki. Hide the book somewhere safe, and for heaven's sake take care. Promise?'

'I promise, Gran. I'll let you know how it goes. Bye for now.' Vicki put the phone down. She couldn't wait to hear what Belper would . . .

But he'd gone.

Table twelve was deserted.

'He had a short fuse, that chap,' said Eileen. 'He went red in the face when you kept him waiting – even his bald head turned pink. Was he really from the council?'

Vicki shook her head. 'No, definitely not.' She went over to the table. There was some change lying on it. Five pounds – more than enough for six glasses of water.

Whatever else Mr Belper was, he wasn't a thief.

That evening Peter turned up later than Vicki had expected. Very much later.

'My parents,' he said apologetically. 'They insisted on playing a few hands of rummy with me. Supposedly because it's my birthday holiday, but I think it's really because they don't like it when I develop interests they know nothing about.' Then, looking around the restaurant, he said, 'I'm beginning to feel really at home here.'

'Have you eaten yet?' Vicki asked. When he shook his head, she went on in an exaggeratedly grown-up voice, 'What a fortunate coincidence. I reserved us a table.'

It was number nineteen, one of Frank's tables. He waited on them like proper customers, lit the candle on the table, enquired what *la bella signorina* would like in the way of *antipasti*, addressed Peter as *Signore*, and was as courteous, deft and efficient as only he knew how to be.

It was clearly going to be an Italian evening, so they

both chose spaghetti Bolognese, the only Italian dish on the menu. (Vicki made a mental note to mention it to her father sometime.) It was a good feeling when Frank took her order. In the Seashell, she normally took orders instead of giving them.

Then she remembered Belper. 'Somebody's after the first mate's journal,' she said, and she told Peter about her peculiar customer at lunchtime.

'That's weird,' he said. 'But I think your grandmother's right. We should hide that book carefully. Where is it now?'

'Upstairs in my chest of drawers. In the junk drawer.'

'That's the first place anyone would look. We need to think of somewhere safer,' Peter said as Frank put the bowls of spaghetti Bolognese down in front of them.

Peter twirled his spaghetti into a ball with his fork. He didn't do it on his spoon, like Vicki, but on the edge of his plate, which made him look very cool. 'I read a story once,' he said, 'about a guy who wanted to hide a letter from the police. No matter how cunning a hiding place he chose, he knew for sure they'd find it in the end, so what did he do?' Peter stopped twirling. 'He hid the letter where the cops would never think of looking.'

'Like where?'

'The place where he kept his other letters. He put it in

with the rest of his post, and it never occurred to the police to look there.'

'I see.' Vicki thought for a moment. 'I could make a brown paper cover for it, the way I do for all my school-books, and then—'

'You put brown paper covers on them all?' Peter stared at her in astonishment.

'Yes,' said Vicki. 'So what?' But she knew it was odd of her. Nobody else in her class did that, but then, none of them wanted to go to sea like she did. Neatness and tidiness were the first commandment on board ship. In an emergency you had to be able to rely on everything working properly. She'd even put dust jackets on her *Hornblower* books, but she didn't tell Peter that. 'If the journal's covered,' she said, 'I could tuck it away among all my other books.'

Peter nodded. 'Right. And Belper could search till he was blue in the face.'

'You really think he'd sneak into my room?'

'Why not? How do you know he isn't searching it right now?'

Belper hadn't done anything of the kind, thank goodness – and, anyway, it seemed pretty unlikely.

But Vicki felt a bit uneasy all the same. The lock on her

bedroom door was a joke – anyone with five fingers on each hand could easily have picked it with a bent safety pin – so she quickly made a paper cover for the journal and put it on her bookshelf. Before that, Peter had quickly skimmed through it. He showed Vicki what was written at the foot of the title page – *Anno Domini MDCCLXXIV* – and said reverently, 'Think of it, printed in 1774. I'm not going to read it right away – not tonight, when we're just about to go aboard the *Storm Goddess*. I'm too excited. Besides,' he confessed, 'I'm scared stiff.'

So was Vicki, although she couldn't bring herself to admit it like he had.

'Can you play rummy?' he asked. She shook her head, so he said, 'Come on, I'll show you.'

They went down to the restaurant and asked Eileen for a pack of cards. Vicki quickly mastered the rules. It was a simple but absorbing game, just the thing to take their minds off what lay ahead.

Later, when the Seashell closed, they went on playing upstairs, not in Vicki's room but in the guest room assigned to Peter. That way, her father couldn't hear that they were still awake.

It was nearly two in the morning when Vicki went to the door, opened it quietly, and listened. Then she shut the door and said, 'I think we can go now.'

*   *   *

The sky had clouded over, and Vicki and Peter were buffeted by the wind when they reached the top of the quay. The bay was bathed in brilliant moonlight whenever the clouds were blown apart, but never for long, and the subsequent darkness seemed even darker.

Vicki had a torch in her pocket and Peter had brought one, too, but they'd agreed not to use them while crossing the mud flats because the light could have been seen for miles. In any case, they could see their target whenever the bay was briefly flooded with moonlight.

The *Storm Goddess* loomed up in the middle of the bay, looking much bigger than she did in daylight. Her sails were flapping in the gusting winds.

She looked as if she was adrift in a heavy sea.

Vicki and Peter didn't run, exactly, but they didn't dawdle either, so it wasn't long before they got close enough to the ship to make out the details.

'What's that over there?' Peter asked suddenly, coming to a halt. He pointed to something on the starboard side of the ship. 'Outside the fence, I mean?'

Vicki could also see it now. 'He did it!'

'Who did what?'

'Phil. He must have got permission to set up his fish and chip stand near the ship.'

Cautiously, they crept towards the fence. They didn't really expect anyone to be outside at this hour, but it was better to be safe than sorry.

They reached the fence without meeting anyone. Naturally. There was no one around but them.

At that moment the ship was brightly lit by another roving shaft of moonlight. 'There it is,' Vicki whispered involuntarily. 'The rope ladder's still there.'

'OK, let's go.' Peter was whispering too. 'Over the fence.'

It surprised them both how easily they got over it. Luckily, the top of the chain-link fence wasn't topped with barbed wire or spikes. Vicki put one foot in Peter's clasped hands, then climbed on his shoulders and scaled the fence easily. Peter followed her, using her hand to help pull himself up. Then they both jumped to the ground.

Vicki straightened up. And that was when she saw him.

He was over near Phil's trailer. She caught only a momentary glimpse of him before he disappeared behind it, and she might not have spotted him at all but for the reflection.

The reflection of the moonlight on his bald head.

Vicki dropped to her knees. 'Belper,' she hissed, pulling Peter down beside her. 'He's over there behind the trailer.'

'Shoot! What's he doing here?'

'He wants to get on board,' Vicki whispered. 'Just like us.'

She looked around. 'Let's go aft. We'll be out of sight there.'

They darted along the ship's side to the stern.

'What now?' Peter whispered. 'Did he see us?'

'He must have, but I don't think he knows we saw *him*.'

'That's no good. We can't climb aboard with him watching.'

Vicki nodded. 'We'll sit tight.'

It was enough to drive her mad! These reporters kept getting in her way. Then she remembered that Belper wasn't a reporter at all. So what was he, and why did he want to get on to the ship?

She *had* to get on to the *Storm Goddess*. It was expected of her. I'll do it, she told herself. Definitely, but I can't do it now.

And then she heard voices.

They were coming from the ship. From the stern cabin overhead – the captain's cabin.

They were men's voices. Two men were talking at once; arguing, quarrelling together in low but heated tones.

Vicki looked at Peter, who nodded. He could hear what she was hearing.

At first she couldn't catch what the men were saying, just the word 'doubloons', which was repeated several times.

Suddenly, one of the men roared, 'Where are they, those doubloons?!' He had a deep, booming voice. 'You had no right to take them, you and your cronies. Where have you hidden them?!'

'I won't tell you!' the other man shouted back. He sounded younger. 'That gold isn't rightfully ours. It'll be the ruin of us!'

All at once, Vicki understood. What was it the first mate had written in his journal?

. . . *fifteen hundred gold doubloons.*

'For the last time: where are those doubloons?!'

'You can search the ship from stem to stern!' shouted the younger man. 'You'll never find them!' A chair scraped on the deck.

'Come back here!' yelled the man with the deep voice. A door slammed. 'Come back, you dog!' There was a clatter, then the door slammed again.

Noises were now coming from overhead. More doors slammed, footsteps raced across the deck. Then came a sudden gunshot.

It wasn't all that loud, but was so unexpected that it pierced Vicki like a knife.

'Come on, men, to arms!' yelled the man with the booming voice. 'Show these cowardly mutineers! Save your gold!'

'On deck, all who fear God and the law!' shouted the younger man. 'Show these lawbreakers! Save the ship!'

At once the deck resounded with a multitude of hurrying footsteps. A babble of voices arose, mingled with the dull thud of blows and the clash of steel on steel.

Then came another gunshot, as muffled as the first but followed by a single cry so agonized and prolonged that Vicki clapped her hands over her ears.

She had seen plenty of films involving pirates and sea battles. In films, a fight on board a ship was a chaotic hurly-burly accompanied by incessant shouting and yelling.

There was shouting on board the *Storm Goddess*, too, but mostly in the form of isolated, spine-chilling cries.

And there were gunshots. Although not as loud as the pistol or musket shots in a film, they sounded just as lethal, perhaps because they rang out singly and were followed by those awful cries.

From time to time there came a sudden yell from many throats at once, a sudden clatter of steel and flurry of blows. And those shouts, that din of battle, sounded more horrific, more brutal and savage, than anything Vicki had ever heard in any film.

Then silence fell again, but not completely. Men were moving around, opening and closing hatches, and if Vicki held her breath she could hear *their* heavy breathing.

Sharply, another cry rang out . . .

A fight was in progress.

A *real* fight.

And it was going on overhead, aboard the *Storm Goddess*.

Vicki looked at Peter. He was staring up at the ship wide-eyed, but nothing on deck could be seen from here, below the stern.

The din gradually subsided. No more shouting, no more heavy breathing, no hatches being opened and closed. No footsteps moving around.

No . . . there *were* footsteps.

Then a sudden crash.

Someone had flung open a hatch.

The man with the booming voice said, 'Cornered you at last, you traitor!'

'What of your gold?' retorted the younger man. 'Have you found it?'

'I'll find it yet. But first I shall dispatch you on your final voyage. I see you've already packed your bundle for the journey, you mutinous dog, so go to the devil!'

Everything happened very quickly after that. There was a patter of footsteps, a metallic clatter, and a long-drawn-out 'Aarrgh!' Something heavy hit the deck with a muffled thud, then silence fell.

'Go to the devil yourself,' said the other man.

His receding footsteps could clearly be heard, then they stopped.

Suddenly, he cried, 'Who called me?' He sounded infinitely surprised. Then a pistol shot rang out.

Vicki and Peter froze.

From the deck came another muffled thud, followed by a long sigh.

Silence.

A deathly hush.

Vicki looked at Peter. She would never have guessed what a comfort it would be to have someone with her. Someone living.

'Come on,' Peter whispered, 'let's get out of here.'

She nodded.

But then they heard the siren.

Grogan and Willis were racing across the mud flats in their police car, lights flashing and siren wailing. Although not particularly loud, the shots aboard the *Storm Goddess* must have carried far across the bay.

The car pulled up beside the gate in the fence, and a spotlight came on. The beam roamed to and fro, then played over the *Storm Goddess*, but there was nothing to be seen. Grogan and Willis got out. Vicki now saw that they had a ladder strapped to the roof of their vehicle. A ladder long enough to reach the deck amidships. Grogan unlocked the gate.

The two men evidently thought the rope ladder might be unsafe, because they propped their ladder against the hull and climbed aboard that way.

Vicki and Peter listened, hardly daring to breathe.

They heard the policemen stomping back and forth on deck, heard them opening and closing hatches and going up and down the companionways. At last the two men came to a halt and conferred in low voices, then climbed back down the ladder. Grogan spoke into his police radio:

'Absolutely no one there, sir. Not a soul on board the ship or anywhere near it . . . yes, I heard it, too, but there's nobody here, believe me . . . certainly, of course I'll keep my eyes peeled, but . . . yes, er, naturally, that goes without saying. OK, sir, good night.' Grogan lowered his radio and glared up at the *Storm Goddess*. 'This was all I needed,' he growled. 'As if I didn't have enough on my plate already.'

'You reckon there's someone behind this?' Willis asked.

'No idea. But if there is, I'll get them, as sure as my name's Tom Grogan.'

PART TWO
THE SHIP

SECOND PROLOGUE

The first mate was sitting with his back propped against the mast. It was all he could do to stay upright, so he'd spread his legs and stretched them out for support. He knew he wouldn't last long if he keeled over. His body would drain like an upended barrel. A barrel filled with lifeblood.

He was young for a ship's officer – not more than twenty-five. His hair was braided into a pigtail, and his tanned face was clean-shaven. He kept his head up and avoided looking down. He could guess that his linen shirt was white no longer. It had been torn open, like his chest. A pistol bullet fired at a range of less than twenty feet had punched a hole in his body the size of a man's fist. It was a miracle it hadn't gone right through. He could feel it lodged inside him. The pain was so great, he could hear himself moaning and groaning, but he didn't care. He would have endured all the pain in the world, provided it didn't spell his death.

He had no wish to die.

He was afraid of death.

No, that was wrong. He was afraid, not of death, but of

what awaited him thereafter. He didn't know exactly what awaited him, only that it would be terrible. So terrible, he would wish himself back here once more, leaning against the mast with this wound in his chest, tormented by pain and faced with the prospect . . . no, that was just it. Faced with the prospect not of being truly dead, but of a death that would be only the prelude to something horrible.

But he was still alive.

All the rest were dead.

Most had died below, but quite a few had been struck down here on deck.

Over beside the forward companionway lay the boatswain, his staunchest ally. He had been the first to be hit by a pistol bullet, like himself, and he'd lost a great deal of blood before he died.

Not far away lay the ship's carpenter, killed with his own axe, and beside him, the sailor who had killed him.

And sprawled against the port bulwark lay the giant captain.

There he lay with a cutlass buried in his chest, the man who had brought this disaster upon them – the man for whom death would have been far too mild a punishment.

But he wasn't truly dead, nor were the rest of the crew. In order to undergo the terrible fate in store for them, they would all be reawakened.

But not before the last of them had died.

And the last of them was himself.

That was the salient point. When he died too – and die he would – everyone would have perished in this fight aboard the ship. Everyone without exception.

Was that just?

No, it was not.

This was why he knew that his dying did not herald the end of everything, but the beginning of something terrible.

He wanted to remain alive for as long as possible, to postpone that terrible something.

When it did come, how long would it last?

For all eternity.

Or so he had often heard. Sailors told many stories of ships' crews who had been banished to a terrible limbo that was neither life nor death.

But there were also reports of some who had been let off more lightly. As in life, so in that terrible limbo, there were said to be mitigating factors and special circumstances that held out hopes of deliverance.

It was a chance that could be exploited, but for that you had to be courageous. Courageous enough to face the fact that your doom was inexorable. Then you could take the precaution of dropping an anchor in the world of the living.

The young man sitting propped against the mast in his sea boots and bloodstained shirt had thrown out an anchor of that kind.

Or so he believed, at least.

He even believed that the anchor had taken hold.

Why? Because he had received a sign.

It was the warning cry, the voice that had alerted him to danger.

The voice had been in his head, but it seemed to come from behind him. Since he'd spun around, the bullet's impact had been partly absorbed by the packet in his hands. Only that explained why he was still alive, and why he had been able to throw out the anchor.

The voice in his head had uttered such a piercing, high-pitched cry, it might almost have been real.

With an effort, summoning up all his remaining strength, the young officer turned his head toward the stairway leading to the poop deck. The cry had seemed to come from that direction.

But there was no one to be seen.

He looked straight ahead again.

Had the warning cry come to him, out of the future? A future that might hold out hopes of deliverance?

If so, that deliverance could be a very long time coming. Very long indeed, for those who had been banished to limbo were beyond the bounds of time as measured by the living.

The young man stared into the distance.

That, he pictured to himself, was where the future might lie.

The future from which the warning cry had come. The future that might hold out the promise of salvation.

He could not have guessed how far away that future was.

Many years away.

Two hundred and thirty years, to be precise.

NINE

It was just after ten o'clock when Vicki knocked on Peter's door. He was already dressed, so they went down to breakfast together. As they passed the foot of the attic stairs he paused. 'Can you see the *Storm Goddess* from up there?'

'Yes, from the window in the attic.'

'Is that where you discovered the photo inside the head?' he asked. 'And the book in the trunk?' Vicki nodded. 'Could I see?'

'Sure,' she said. 'As long as my father isn't around.' She listened, but there were no sounds from below. Dad and Eileen usually went shopping for the restaurant at this hour. They were probably out, but one couldn't be sure. 'After breakfast, OK?'

Peter nodded, and they went downstairs.

Dad and Eileen *had* gone out. Lying on the breakfast table was the note Vicki had left there last night: *Went to bed late. Sleeping in.* Underneath, Eileen had scrawled: *Good morning, you night owls!*

Vicki and Peter had talked for hours. At first on their way home across the mud flats – they'd waited for Grogan and Willis to drive off before climbing back over the fence, regardless of whether Belper had seen them – and later in Peter's room.

What had been going on aboard the *Storm Goddess*?

'That argument,' said Peter. 'Those men who were quarrelling – who could they have been?'

Vicki stared at him. That was clear as daylight, wasn't it? Then it occurred to her that Peter still hadn't read the journal. 'Just a minute,' she said. She dashed upstairs to her room, grabbed the little book, and was back in no time. 'Here,' she told him. 'Read the beginning.'

Peter started reading.

It wasn't long before he looked up. 'The captain and his first mate . . . ' he said, staring into space. Then he looked at Vicki. 'The captain and the first mate were quarrelling. Quarrelling over some doubloons.' Slowly, he said, 'In other words, the fifteen hundred gold doubloons the captain had hidden.'

'Exactly,' said Vicki. 'From the sound of it, though, the first mate found them and hid them somewhere else. And the captain wanted to know where.'

Peter nodded. 'And that's how the fight started.'

It had been a fight – a *real* one – that was for sure. But if people of flesh and blood had been fighting, what had become of them? The police couldn't have seen anyone, or they'd have raised the alarm.

'We were lucky,' said Peter. 'Just imagine what might have happened if we'd become mixed up in that fight.'

Vicki shivered. 'I'd rather not.'

'Look . . . ' Peter hesitated. 'The police will be watching the ship like hawks after this. It'll be pretty difficult to get on board . . . think what could happen to us there . . . don't get me wrong, but maybe we should drop the idea?'

That was just how Vicki felt too, but she shook her head. 'I've got to get on to that ship. Somebody's waiting for me—' She broke off. What made her so sure? Where had that certainty come from? No, it wasn't a certainty, just a feeling, and a very hazy feeling at that.

Was it worth putting herself and Peter in danger?

'At least,' she said hesitantly, 'I think they are.'

Peter hadn't pressed her on the subject. 'OK,' he said, 'let's think it over some more.' Then he'd suggested calling it a night.

'I won't be able to sleep, not now!' Vicki protested, but once in bed she fell fast asleep.

Vicki had woken up with a start while it was still dark. At first she couldn't think why. Then she became aware how low she was feeling – how utterly depressed. And then it dawned on her: she'd been dreaming. Dreaming of what? Yes, she remembered it now: the deck of an old sailing ship. She had sensed, rather than known, that she was aboard the *Storm Goddess,* and there were bodies lying everywhere. Dead bodies, beyond a doubt, and sitting with his back against the mast was a man. He'd been gazing at her – gazing at her with an infinitely sorrowful expression . . . and then she'd woken up.

The dream began to fade even as she recalled it, and she realized that it had simply been a product of her experiences during the night. No reason to feel so depressed, she'd told herself.

But the feeling had persisted. It was such a strong sensation, she wondered in retrospect how she'd managed to go back to sleep.

Now that she was sitting at the breakfast table, having caught up on her sleep, she felt easier in her mind. That, of course, was because Peter was there. She couldn't imagine having to cope with the *Storm Goddess*'s secret on her own.

Peter pointed to the TV set on the counter. 'Mind if we turn it on? There may be something about the *Storm Goddess*.'

There was. The TV reporter who'd been in the Seashell two days before was pictured standing in front of the ship. 'Everything is quiet here at present,' he was saying, 'if you discount the numerous sightseers who have turned up again today. Speaking at a press conference earlier this morning, an expert on shipwrecks from the Society for Nautical Research announced the result of scientific tests carried out on the *Storm Goddess*'s timbers to determine their age. These prove beyond doubt that the ship dates from the eighteenth century, but it's still a mystery how she comes to be lying here in the bay. On the other hand, a rational explanation has been found for last night's strange goings-on.

'As we reported earlier, it seemed at first that a fight had broken out on board the *Storm Goddess*. The police failed to find any evidence of this. At the press conference, however, the harbour master introduced an acoustics expert who stated that the empty bay may have functioned like a huge, concave reflector of sound waves. The *Storm Goddess* is situated at its focal point, so it's probable that the sounds heard last night – sounds that may have come from some distant open-air venue showing a pirate film – were collected there like light by a magnifying glass and reflected across the bay. That's all for now from the mysterious *Storm Goddess*. We'll keep you informed of any further developments. And now, back to the studio.'

'Sounds from some open-air venue?' said Vicki. 'Who are they kidding?'

Peter adjusted his glasses. 'It's possible. Technically, I mean.'

'Well, it doesn't wash with me.' Vicki shook her head firmly. 'Besides, it would have been a pretty odd movie.'

'Why?'

'Have *you* ever seen a pirate film without any background music?'

Just then the phone rang.

Vicki went over to the serving counter. 'The Seashell Restaurant,' she said into the phone.

'Is this the boss's daughter?' asked a man's voice. It sounded familiar. Very familiar. 'Is that you, Vicki?'

'Yes, but who's speaking?'

There was a short pause. Then the voice said, 'Inspector Grogan here.'

Vicki gave a start, but quickly recovered herself. 'Hello, Inspector,' she said loudly for Peter's benefit, simultaneously pressing the speakerphone button. Peter stared at her tensely. 'What can I do for you?'

'I'd appreciate it,' said Grogan, 'if you'd come down to the station.'

'What for?'

'It's about the *Storm Goddess*.'

Peter drew a question mark in the air.

'What about the *Storm Goddess*?' asked Vicki.

'I can't tell you over the phone.' Grogan paused. 'Look, I can't force you to come. I really should be speaking to your father, but you'd be wiser to keep him in the dark. Is that plain enough?'

Vicki looked at Peter, who nodded.

'All right,' she said. 'I don't have a clue what you want, but I'll come. I'll be there in half an hour or so.' She hung up the phone. 'Why should I go?' she asked Peter.

'Because it's the only way we'll find out what he wants.'

'We? I'm the only one he asked for.'

'You think I'd let you go there on your own?'

They were about to set off for the police station when Vicki remembered she didn't have her mobile phone with her. She wanted to be available if her father called, so she dashed upstairs to her bedroom and put the phone in her pocket. After a careful look around – was the journal in its proper place? – she went out and locked the door behind

145

her. And then, just as she removed the key, she heard it.

A groan.

She froze, listening intently.

Nothing.

Had she been mistaken? Irresolutely, she made for the stairs. There it was again: someone was groaning. It sounded like a man, and he was somewhere overhead.

She listened.

A man was gasping and groaning upstairs in the attic.

Hadn't Dad gone out? Should she call Peter?

Reluctantly, she made her way to the foot of the attic stairs. She started to climb them, instinctively making as little noise as possible. Halfway up, she paused.

The gasping and groaning had ceased.

Had she misheard?

That was precisely what she wanted to find out. Slowly, she went on climbing, then halted once more.

There it was again, the groaning and laboured breathing. She could locate it for certain now: it was coming from the attic. Was her father looking for something in the old trunk? If so, why would he be groaning?

She thought for a moment, then darted up the rest of the stairs and tiptoed to the door.

No doubt about it, the gasping and groaning was coming from inside. Cautiously, she turned the handle . . . locked!

The door to the attic was locked. Why had Dad locked the door behind him? Stupid question: because he was looking for something in the trunk and didn't want to be disturbed.

She hesitated again. Should she turn back? Should she simply go away? What if something was wrong? What if Dad had collapsed? She'd read only recently that chefs were more prone to heart attacks than other people.

She took the passkey from her pocket and inserted it in the lock, then cautiously turned it. The lock opened without a sound. Gently, she turned the handle.

And there he was.

Vicki went rigid.

It was a man she'd seen before.

The man in last night's dream.

He was sitting propped against the trunk with his sea boots planted far apart on the floor. The front of his white, loose-sleeved shirt was soaked with blood. Vicki looked at his face.

His smooth, clean-shaven cheeks were grey. He was gazing at her.

Vicki almost screamed, but she didn't.

You didn't scream at someone who looked at you this way. Not mournfully, as in last night's dream, but steadily and insistently. He was still gasping for breath, but he wasn't groaning any more.

She stood looking at the stranger with his back propped against the trunk – really and truly sitting there, breathing like any living creature – and she wasn't afraid. She knew he wouldn't harm her. She was about to say something, but he raised his hand and put a finger to his lips.

'Vicki?' she heard suddenly. It was Peter calling her from downstairs. 'Are you coming?'

Vicki hesitated, wondering whether to answer. She kept her eyes fixed on the stranger, but he merely continued to hold her gaze with a finger to his lips, so she went out and quietly shut the door.

Peter was halfway up the stairs to the second floor. 'Where are you, Vicki?'

'I'm here,' she called back.

'Up there?' Peter climbed the attic stairs. 'I thought we were going to the police station.' He looked at the door. 'Is that the attic? Can I see it?'

Vicki nodded and stepped aside.

He opened the door and went in.

Vicki held her breath.

She heard Peter's footsteps on the bare boards, nothing more. Then, after a while, she heard him say, 'It isn't half as creepy as I imagined.'

She followed him in.

The man had vanished.

The floorboards on which he'd been sitting beside the trunk were as spotless as the rest of the room.

But he'd been there in the flesh. She'd seen and heard him.

The first mate of the *Storm Goddess* had appeared to her.

The sun was shining as brightly as it had shone for the last few days. Perfect weather for a swim – or would have been, thought Vicki as she walked along the quay with Peter.

It was three days since the sea had disappeared, and people were beginning to get used to the sight of the waterless bay with an eighteenth-century square-rigged sailing ship lying high and dry at its central point. The *Storm Goddess* was a prime attraction, of course. People came in droves to see an eighteenth-century ship up close. Curiously enough, they seemed unconcerned by the fact that her sudden appearance was utterly inexplicable, if not a total impossibility.

Vicki wondered where the first mate was now.

He had appeared to her. Not merely as a dream figure or a kind of ghost, but as a visible, audible creature of flesh and blood, so he had to be somewhere. But it was pointless to wonder where he was. Why? Because the question was unanswerable. As unanswerable as the question of where the *Storm Goddess* had sprung from overnight.

Vicki could see the sailor in her mind's eye. She could see him leaning back against the trunk with the wound in his chest she'd tried not to look at too closely, his clean-shaven face grey beneath its tan. She could picture his earnest, insistent gaze.

She didn't even have to shut her eyes to summon up this image as she walked along with Peter beside her. Presumably this was quite normal when you were suddenly confronted by a real, live, eighteenth-century sailor. Vicki supposed that the picture would remain with her. But for how long was another unanswerable question. In any case, she didn't mind if the first mate's image persisted.

But one question *did* require an answer: should she tell Peter about the apparition? Vicki thought about this as she accompanied him along the quay to the town hall. The first mate hadn't shown himself to Peter, so she guessed he didn't want him to know.

But she'd let Peter in on all the *Storm Goddess*'s secrets up to this point. He'd been in this with her from the start, and she knew she wouldn't be able to do what she had to do without him. Why should she exclude him now?

Even as she was thinking this, she had another vision of the first mate with a finger to his lips. 'Say nothing!' had been his message in the attic, and the same applied now. This was one secret she couldn't share with Peter. The sailor definitely didn't want him to know.

But it would all be so much simpler if he did. After all, she would need Peter's help in doing what she needed to do . . .

'You're very quiet,' said Peter. 'Anything wrong?'

'I've been thinking. Listen, Peter . . . if I told you I was going to handle this *Storm Goddess* business on my own, what would you say?'

Peter gave her a sidelong look. 'You're planning to have another go at getting on board her, right?'

Vicki nodded.

'Then I'm coming too – that's what I'd say.' After a moment he added, 'You know I'm not too keen on going aboard, but if you think someone's waiting for you, I suppose I'll have to.'

TEN

Vicki had been inside the town hall a few times, but never in the police station. The station turned out to be a room with bare walls painted a frosty shade of sea green. Running across it was a massive counter, and behind this, separated from the general public like a dangerous elephant seal in a zoo, sat Inspector Grogan. Sergeant Willis, who was sitting opposite him, looked rather like a malevolent weasel without his peaked cap.

Grogan got up from his desk. 'Ah, there you are, young lady. Complete with escort, I see.' He lumbered over to the counter. 'Which answers my first question: who else was with you on board the *Storm Goddess* last night?'

'Me? On board the *Storm Goddess* last night?' Vicki shook her head. 'Not me. Whatever gave you that idea?'

She and Peter had agreed to deny everything at first, what-ever they were asked.

'Listen, miss,' said Grogan, breathing heavily, 'you'd better come clean if you want to stay out of trouble. You and your friend were seen.' He paused for effect, or so he hoped. 'Seen by me and my colleague here.'

Vicki was momentarily taken aback. Could that be true? If so, why hadn't Grogan shouted, 'Hey, come here, the two of you!' or something like that?

Because the cops hadn't seen them at all, that was why! She and Peter had been so well hidden by the ship, they *couldn't* have seen them. In that case, who had?

Belper!

Belper must have told on them.

But why? And why hadn't Grogan said so?

In any case, it was pointless to deny it now.

'Well, OK,' Vicki said, 'we did go and have a look, just for fun. It's not against the law, is it?'

'No,' someone said abruptly, '*that* isn't.'

It was the harbour master, who had entered without a sound. How long had he been listening? 'Come with me,' he said, towering over Vicki and Peter. 'Both of you.'

He strode on ahead, clearly not worried that they might try to give him the slip, and they followed him up the stairs to his office in the nearby town hall. 'Have a seat,' he said, jerking his head at two chairs in front of his desk. The desk and the leather swivel chair behind it were as huge as the harbour master himself. Vicki and Peter felt like pygmies in a land of giants.

'Right,' said the harbour master, 'now let's talk like reasonable people.' He folded his huge paws on his stomach. 'You were seen near the ship, but not by Grogan and Willis.' He assumed a buddy-buddy smile which said, *Look, I'm treating you like equals*.

Vicki and Peter stared at him blankly.

The smile vanished. 'I'm not going to tell you who saw you.' He paused. Abruptly he asked, 'What were you after on the *Storm Goddess*?'

'We weren't planning to go on board the ship,' said Peter, looking as innocent as a newborn lamb. 'It's out of bounds, isn't it?'

'Now listen here, youngster – what's your name, by the way? Peter? Good, now listen here, Peter – you, too, Vicki. You wanted to get aboard, that's an established fact. For all I know, you *did* get aboard, so listen carefully.' The harbour master leaned forward and glared at them. 'The *Storm Goddess* isn't just closed to the general public, it's an object of the greatest scientific interest. If anything on board turns out to have been moved or damaged, *you'll* be held respon-sible. And then, Vicki, your father will pay through the nose. And so will your parents,' he added, turning to Peter.

Vicki avoided looking at Peter because the harbour master might have believed that his threat had impressed her in some way – which it had.

'But we weren't on board anyway,' Vicki said. 'Grogan and Willis were,' she added. 'They may have moved or damaged something.'

'*Inspector* Grogan and *Sergeant* Willis to you!' The harbour master glowered at her. 'They took the greatest care, naturally. The police never move or damage things, young lady, so get that straight.' He sat back in his chair. 'And now here's some friendly advice: if you tell me what you were after on board that ship, I'll forget you were ever there.'

Once again, Vicki carefully avoided glancing at Peter. That would have looked like a signal, and she had no need to send him one. What mattered now was to admit nothing. All she could say was, 'We can't tell you what we were doing on board because we didn't go on board and never planned to.'

'That's fine,' said the harbour master, in a tone that conveyed the opposite. 'Then we'll play it another way. I'll send for your parents and tell them what their little darlings get up to late at night. And I'll advise them to put plenty of money aside to cover the cost of repairs to the

Storm Goddess. Until they get here, I'll have to ask Inspector Grogan to lock you up for safety's sake.'

Vicki was transfixed with terror. This was it. Her father would learn that she'd been doing things behind his back. He trusted her, so he'd be bitterly disappointed. Not only that, but he'd probably ground her for a month – and she *had* to get on board the *Storm Goddess*. The first mate was waiting . . . and Peter? What would his parents say? She glanced at him after all. He'd turned pale and was biting his lower lip.

'Oh, sorry, am I intruding?'

Rose Redd was standing in the doorway. She had entered without knocking.

'Am I too early for our interview?' she asked brightly. She shut the door behind her and walked across the room. 'Oh!' she said, coming to a halt. 'Did I forget to knock? How embarrassing. Many apologies, harbour master.'

'That's all right,' said the harbour master. 'Would you mind waiting outside for a moment?'

'Not at all.' She walked back to the door, where she paused and turned. 'By the way,' she said, 'what was that I happened to overhear? You're going to have them locked up?' She retraced her steps and planted herself in front of the harbour master's desk, a slim, erect, auburn-haired figure. 'Throwing a couple of children into the cells?

Really, harbour master! You can't do that, you know it as well as I do, whatever they've been up to.' She smiled at Vicki. Then she said casually, 'But you weren't being serious, naturally. You were only trying to scare them, right?'

'Er . . . of course, Miss Redd. OK,' he growled at Vicki and Peter. 'You can go, but don't think you've heard the last of this. We've got some unfinished business to settle.'

'So have we,' said Rose, sitting down in the chair Vicki had just left. 'Our business is very far from unfinished, isn't it, harbour master?'

Vicki and Peter waited outside the town hall for Rose Redd to emerge. They went over to her.

'Thanks,' said Vicki. She hesitated, then added, 'I'm sure he wasn't really planning to have us locked up. Not seriously, I mean.'

'That would have taken the biscuit,' said Rose. 'Wrongful imprisonment, it's called.' She looked at Vicki. 'Did you, or didn't you, go on board that ship?'

'We didn't.' Vicki raised her right hand. 'Scouts' honour.'

'So we couldn't have done any damage,' said Peter. 'But he plans to make our parents pay anyway.'

Rose shook her head. 'Forget it.'

'Why?'

'Because I told him to leave you alone.'

'Oh, right,' said Vicki. 'You mean he does exactly what you tell him?'

'Yes. He thinks I know something about him, something important, and he's scared I'll write an article about it.'

'Do you? Know something important, I mean?'

Rose shrugged. 'Maybe, maybe not.' She pointed to a bench on the quay. 'Shall we?'

They went over to it and sat down, with Rose in the middle. She held out her hand to Vicki. 'Truce?' And, when Vicki hesitated, 'I don't mean you any harm. I simply want to find out what's going on.'

'Yes,' said Vicki, 'and then write about it – and me.'

'I won't even mention your name, if you don't want me to.' Rose turned to Peter. 'Nor yours. Besides, I still don't know if I'll use what you tell me.' She looked from one to the other. 'You *are* going to tell me something, I suppose?'

Vicki and Peter leaned forward and looked at each other.

'Why not?' said Peter. 'I vote we tell her the whole story.'

Vicki straightened up. She'd meant to say 'OK,' but something had occurred to her. 'We'll tell you everything, but only if you answer a question first.'

'That depends on the question. Let's hear it.'

'Rose Redd . . . is that your real name?'

The reporter laughed. 'Don't you like it? I do. Everyone

wonders the same thing. It lends me an air of mystery.' She turned serious. 'Is that really your condition?'

'No,' Vicki replied. 'I'd simply like to know the answer.'

'And I'd prefer to leave the question open.' Rose looked from Vicki to Peter. 'I've got a suggestion. Just call me Rose, OK?'

'OK, Rose,' said Vicki and Peter.

The restaurant was busier than it had been in ages. Everyone seemed to have arranged to lunch in the Seashell, not only the families with little children, but all the sightseers attracted to the town by the *Storm Goddess*. And today, of all days, Dad's assistant chef was off sick.

'Miss! Where's our order?'

'Coming right away!' called Vicki. She knew it would be quite a while before the order arrived, but you couldn't tell customers 'Sorry, one of our chefs is sick.' They might think something was wrong with the food and decide never to come back.

Eileen usually kept the hatch to the kitchen open, but not today. 'They're busy enough in there as it is,' she said. 'No need for them to hear the customers grumbling on top of everything else.' But the waiters heard them, Vicki included, and it really annoyed her, especially today.

Now that she'd actually seen the first mate – she still had

159

a vivid recollection of his earnest, searching gaze – how could she be expected to worry about some impatient customer demanding his fillet of plaice?

Naturally, she had said nothing to Rose about the sailor's appearance. Nor about the fact that she and Peter were sure they'd heard a genuine fight in progress last night. Like everyone else, apparently, Rose believed that the sound had come from a pirate film, and Vicki and Peter hadn't said otherwise.

Lunchtime seemed to go on for ever today. Vicki's manner became more and more sullen and unfriendly. She was starting to feel almost as low as she'd felt during the night. When she was finally allowed to knock off at three – partly, no doubt, because Eileen had noticed her mood – she felt like a bird released from its cage.

Just then, Peter appeared in the Seashell. Vicki couldn't have been more delighted if she hadn't seen him for days. 'Hi, Peter!' she called with a beaming smile, and waited for him to smile back.

But he merely gave her a thoughtful nod and said, 'I realized something. Something about this morning.' He looked around the restaurant. 'Could we go up to your room?'

'Sure.' Vicki led the way upstairs. Her bedroom was in semi-darkness because the blind was still down. It went whirring up as she released it.

Peter joined her at the window and opened it. 'You can see the quay from here.' He went over to Vicki's desk and sat down. 'The thing is,' he said, 'it occurred to me that—'

'Wait a minute,' Vicki said, and shut the window. 'Just in case . . .'

'It's the harbour master,' Peter began again. 'Didn't something he said strike you as odd?'

Vicki thought for a moment, then shook her head.

'It did to me,' said Peter. 'He asked what we were "after" on board the *Storm Goddess*.'

'Yes, well, I suppose he wanted to know what we had in mind.'

'That's what I thought, too, at first. But just now, as I was passing the town hall on my way here, I remembered the *way* he said it.' Peter paused. 'He wanted to know what we were *looking for*. He thinks we're after something that's hidden on board.' He looked at Vicki. 'What could it be?'

He hadn't finished, Vicki could tell. She was surprised it hadn't occurred to him, perhaps because he . . .

'But of course!' He slapped his forehead. 'It's the gold – the fifteen hundred doubloons!'

Vicki nodded. 'The only thing is, how does he know about it?'

Suddenly Peter raised one finger. 'Belper! That's who

told him. Belper must have heard the captain and the first mate quarrelling over it.'

But Vicki shook her head. 'I think Belper knew about the gold already. Why else would he have gone out to the ship?'

'True, but *how* did he know about it?'

'Good question.' Vicki took the first mate's journal from the bookshelf. 'He doesn't know what's in here, so how else?'

Peter thought for a moment. Then he said, 'We ought to tell Rose about this. Maybe something will occur to her.'

Vicki nodded. 'I'll call her.' She reached for her mobile phone.

Just then Peter's mobile rang. He fished it out of his jeans pocket. 'Yes? *What?* But why? – Can't you go by yourselves?' He held the phone away from his ear, and Vicki could hear a woman's voice yakking away, a rather shrill voice. 'OK, OK,' Peter said. 'Where shall we meet? – It's a ship, not a boat. – No, Mum, I'm not trying to be rude. – OK, see you.' He pocketed the phone and shook his head. 'Now they want to go for a walk with me across the mud flats to the *Storm Goddess*.' He mimicked his mother's voice: '"And, if possible, without that little friend of yours."' He seemed really angry, but then he shrugged. 'Sorry, Vicki, there's nothing I can do.'

Vicki shrugged too. It was no use wishing a hurricane would blow his parents off to the Costa del Sol. They would be bound to scoop him up and take him with them. 'I'll walk some of the way with you,' she said.

She replaced the journal on the shelf, and they left the room. Vicki locked the door. 'We'll go out the back way,' she said. 'Then you can see the kitchen.'

They walked along the hallway that led to the back door. The kitchen door was open as usual. Her father was toiling over one of the stoves with his back to them, juggling with several pots and pans at once. His chef's hat was over one eye – in violation of one of his own strict rules.

Hastily, Vicki yanked Peter away from the door. Dad was obviously stressed. No need to bother him just when he might explode and start rampaging around the kitchen.

Vicki accompanied Peter along the quay until his parents came into view in the distance, then said goodbye.

Next, she called Rose and told her that Belper was after the gold. Rose said nothing, just whistled through her teeth.

'We're wondering how he found out about it,' Vicki went on. 'I mean, he doesn't know about the first mate's journal.'

'I'd like to look at that sometime,' said Rose.

'Of course. As soon as I've finished reading it myself.'

'How did you discover that Belper was after the gold?'

Vicki told her.

'Just a moment.' Rose's voice betrayed sudden excitement. 'You think the harbour master knows about it as well? That means he and Belper are in it together!'

Vicki hadn't looked at it that way, but it made sense. 'I suppose you're right,' she said.

Rose gave another whistle. 'I think I'd better try to find out who this so-called reporter really is. If he and the harbour master really are in this together—' She broke off. 'Incidentally, Vicki, I've heard your father wants to buy the Seashell.'

'That's right, he does.'

'So why doesn't he?'

'Because the harbour master won't sell. Dad says he's simply being mean.'

'I see.' Rose left it at that.

Afterwards, Vicki spent a while standing on the coast road above the spot where Phil's fish and chip stand had been until yesterday, looking out across the mud flats. There lay the *Storm Goddess* with her masts jutting skyward and sightseers milling around the fence that enclosed her. The crowd was particularly thick near the fish and chip stand's new site. Where Phil was concerned, the *Storm Goddess*'s presence seemed to be paying off.

The same went for Captain Ahab, who had erected a sign by the town hall on the quay. 'Musical mystery tour!' it read. 'Visit the *Storm Goddess* with an old sea dog who can tell you what life was really like on board a sailing ship!' Vicki estimated that Captain Ahab and his band had attracted at least fifty paying customers, most of them children.

She made her way back to the Seashell.

There were a lot of cars parked outside – many more than was usual at this time of the afternoon. The restaurant, too, seemed to be profiting from the *Storm Goddess*'s presence.

Vicki left the path along the quay, intending to go in by the back door.

And then, just as she emerged from behind one of the parked cars, she saw him.

He was rounding the corner of the restaurant, eyes darting this way and that, bald head glistening in the afternoon sunshine.

It was Belper.

ELEVEN

Vicki darted behind the parked car and crouched down.

What if Belper had sneaked into the building, forced open her bedroom door, and stolen the journal?

She heard his footsteps approaching. They passed the car she was hiding behind, and she saw him walk off down the road.

Should she shout? Should she raise the alarm?

But, wait a minute, maybe he hadn't found the book at all.

She dashed over to the restaurant, in through the back door, past the kitchen, and upstairs to her room.

The door was locked! Swiftly, she opened it and hurried over to the bookshelf.

And there it was.

The slim volume was still there, sandwiched between her school books.

Or was it?

Vicki pulled it out and opened it.

Journal kept by
the FIRST MATE
of the 'Storm Goddess'

Phew!

She went over to the door, then halted. Could Belper have unlocked and locked the door behind him with a skeleton key so that she wouldn't notice a thing? Or had he never been inside the room at all?

Her telescope! She'd put it back in her odds-and-ends drawer. On the right-hand side – she remembered that distinctly. She hurried over and wrenched the drawer open.

The telescope was on the left-hand side.

Vicki closed the drawer. Why was Belper so set on finding the first mate's journal?

However he'd found out, he obviously knew about the fifteen hundred gold doubloons – the treasure that must be hidden somewhere on board the *Storm Goddess*. What else did he hope to learn from the book? What other information could it contain?

But of course!

It was clear as daylight.

Belper wanted to find out *where* the gold was hidden. He assumed that the first mate had revealed the hiding place in his journal, that must be why the book meant so much to him.

Vicki got out her mobile. She couldn't wait to tell Peter how well his hiding-place idea had worked. But then she remembered that he was out on the mud flats with his parents. It might be wiser not to intrude. She pocketed her phone again.

What if the first mate really did say where the gold was hidden? Quickly, she took out the book again and sat down at her desk. A shame this wasn't the original text – she was curious to know what the first mate's handwriting looked like. On the other hand, she might not have been able to read his old-fashioned script very easily, so perhaps it was a good thing, after all, that the journal had been reproduced in print. She opened the book at the page she'd reached before.

Vicki had a vision of the sailor's face, of his grave, searching expression, and wondered how old he'd been. She found it hard to judge the ages of grown-ups, especially men with beards, but the first mate was clean-shaven. For that reason, and because everything else about him gave that impression, she felt pretty sure he was much younger than her father. Not as young as Peter, of course, but far closer to his age than to Dad's.

How could things have come to such a pass? I must render an account of myself. I have time enough, for the wind has dropped entirely.

To think what a happy, contented man I was in the early summer of this year, when I was still serving as petty officer on the Gertrude . . .

She stopped. She hadn't locked the door. She walked over to it and turned the key twice in the lock, then read on.

But then came the day when that giant of a captain appeared.

No one knew him. He was reputed to be a stranger who had prospered mightily and merited respect on that account.

The captain came as a passenger aboard a cotton-carrying merchantman that anchored in the harbour not far from the Gertrude. *He had himself rowed ashore together with two dark-skinned men attired in colourful, outlandish clothes. The townsfolk marvelled at these men.*

They marvelled likewise when the captain had several mysterious chests brought ashore. These chests seemed exceptionally heavy. What, everyone wondered, could be concealed in them?

At the time of which I write, there was for sale in the town a very handsome inn with a lofty, spacious ballroom. It now became clear that the captain was rightly considered wealthy. He purchased the inn on the spot, paying the full asking price in good Spanish gold doubloons.

In the meantime, something else became known. It transpired, when the deed of sale was drawn up, that the captain was no stranger at all, but the only son of a fisherman and his wife who had met an untimely death, whereupon the boy, being a penniless orphan, had been consigned to the poorhouse. Although his parentage would ordinarily have destined him to become a fisherman, he disliked the notion and rebelled against it. Being exceptionally big and strong for his age, even as a lad, he formed the idea of running away to sea. One day, when he was still a mere stripling, he absconded from the poorhouse and disappeared. No one shed any tears over him.

All these things became the talk of the town, and the captain was regarded with new eyes. An impoverished fisherman's son! A person of low degree! Was it right that such a man should acquire a handsome inn? Did he deserve his wealth? People whispered together, wagged their heads, and wrinkled their noses at the upstart.

None of this seemed to disturb the captain. He announced that the inn would be closed for a spell but reopened in a few weeks' time, its interior having been refurbished in a fashion that *would cause universal astonishment.*

The townsfolk shrugged their shoulders at this.

The captain had the chests he'd brought with him carried into the inn. He thereupon closeted himself in the building, together with the two dark-skinned men and all manner of materials required for plastering and painting walls, and was not seen again for days on end.

No one thought anything of this at first. However, when the captain remained shut up in the inn for several weeks and had his meals brought to the door, people became curious as to what he and his servants were doing in there. Meanwhile, the windows had been carefully protected against prying eyes with wooden shutters, a circumstance that only whetted people's interest still more.

But at last, when their curiosity had become almost unendurable, it was announced that all the town's inhabitants, high and low, young and old, were invited to inspect the inn's newly refurbished ballroom on the last Sunday of July.

They all came. And all were amazed beyond measure.

Every wall of the spacious ballroom had been plastered anew and covered with seashells. There were large shells and small, smooth and fluted, white and coloured, dull and lustrous, round and elongated. Some hailed from the Atlantic and others from the South Seas (the latter being in the majority), and all had been embedded in the plaster with their curved sides facing outward. Diverse in the extreme, they included great scallop shells, tiny mussel shells, jagged oyster shells, and all manner of tropical cockleshells.

No one had ever seen such a sight before.

The tall sea captain, who stood lording it in the middle of the room, savoured his guests' admiration – or so he thought. In reality, they were in tacit agreement that this Seashell Room (for so they promptly christened it) was grossly overdone and every inch the handiwork of a self-important upstart. What added to this impression was that the captain, in his vainglory, had hung a portrait of himself at one end of the room. Although this picture bore a remarkable resemblance to himself, it had been crudely executed in oils, doubtless by one of his servants.

These two dark-skinned men were not present when the Seashell room was inaugurated, nor were they ever seen again. It was rumoured that they had secretly embarked on a West Indiaman and returned to their native land.

A few days later—

Vicki stared into space.

So that was how the Seashell Room had come into being!

172

She jumped up and went to the door, but first replaced the journal among her books. Then she ran downstairs to the restaurant.

It was still busy, but that didn't matter now. Leaning against the counter, Vicki surveyed the shell-encrusted walls.

'What are you looking at?' Eileen asked.

'I'm trying to imagine how someone would have felt walking into this room for the first time two hundred and thirty years ago.'

'Two hundred and thirty years ago? Before there were TV sets, magazines, or movies?' Eileen looked around. 'They'd have been bowled over, I should think.' She gave an emphatic nod.

That was more or less what Vicki thought. All the same, the townsfolk had turned up their noses. The captain must have found that really galling.

In his place, she would have paid them back in some way.

She looked up at the captain's portrait. The tourist brochure said it had little artistic merit. This meant absolutely nothing to her, but if the picture looked even a little bit like him, the captain hadn't been a handsome man. His face was pitted, as if the sea had eaten it away, and it wore a spiteful, contemptuous smile. This, Vicki saw, was because his eyes weren't smiling like his lips. They were narrowed in a menacing way, and his evil, mocking smile was directed at the place on the opposite wall that was normally occupied by the Storm Goddess's head. Looking at the picture, Vicki felt for the first time that it was really rather frightening.

If an ability to inspire fear was a sign of a good picture, then the captain's portrait wasn't so bad after all. Vicki returned to her bedroom.

A few days later the giant captain appeared on board the Gertrude. *What he was doing there I was soon to find out. In company with the other ship's officers, I was summoned to the mess, where our own captain, a genial old soul, informed all present—*

'Hello?' Vicki's mobile had rung.

'Hi, Vicki. It's Peter. I just thought of something.'

'Aren't you out at the *Storm Goddess* with your parents?'

'Yes, but they're treating themselves to some fish and chips at Phil's trailer. I told them I needed the loo.'

Vicki giggled. 'With all those people around? Where?'

'Shows what you know! They've set up a whole row of Portaloos and parked a camper van inside the fence. The police are moving into it. Looks like they'll be guarding the ship around the clock from now on.'

Oh no, thought Vicki. How will we get on to the ship now?

'Don't worry,' she heard Peter say, 'we'll get on board somehow.' That didn't solve the problem, of course, but in some strange way she felt better.

She told him that Belper had managed to get into her room but that, thanks to Peter's bright idea, he'd failed to find the book. 'D'you know what he was looking for?'

'Of course I do,' said Peter. 'He thinks the first mate described where the gold is hidden.' He laughed. 'That's what I thought of – that's why I called you.'

And why *she* had meant to call *him*. That was more than a coincidence. It wasn't telepathy, exactly, but it meant that she and Peter were still on the same wavelength. She'd been afraid things between them would be different now, since she hadn't told him about seeing the sailor in the attic.

'Know what I'd like to know?' she heard him say.

'No idea.' After all, being on the same wavelength didn't make you a mind-reader.

'I'd like to know where those fifteen hundred doubloons came from.'

Same here, thought Vicki.

'My parents are coming! Got to go. Bye.' And he hung up.

Vicki sighed and went back to reading the journal.

In company with the other ship's officers, I was summoned to the mess, where our own captain, a genial old soul, informed all present that the Gertrude had a new owner, the giant captain.

I was thoroughly dismayed, I must confess, for I realized at once that our skipper's humane regime was a thing of the past.

The captain had leased the Seashell Room for a good rent and now proposed to go trading in the Gertrude. He acted without delay. He dismissed half the crew and all the officers save me, whom he reappointed first mate (to my misfortune, I cannot refrain from adding as I write these words).

He thereupon hired new hands and officers, and it was remarkable how speedily he found them. I gained the impression that many of the new men were scoundrels of one kind or another (ah, if only I had followed my instincts and signed off!). From now on, there were two opposing and roughly equal camps aboard the Gertrude: the remnants of the original crew, and those who had just signed on.

And then, three days before we sailed, the Gertrude was renamed.

The captain was well within his rights to do this, but why, of all names, did he have to settle on Storm Goddess?

The old hands, who immediately construed that appellation as a portent of disaster, grumbled at it, whereupon the captain mustered all hands and announced that two regulations were now in force on board.

In the first place, each member of the crew would receive, in addition to his normal pay, a share of any future profits gained by trade, these to be allotted in accordance with the rank of the man in question. The crew greeted this announcement with three hearty cheers.

Secondly, however, any form of insubordination, even a muttered word of complaint, would henceforth be punished unmercifully with thirty lashes. This aroused . . .

[Illegible]

These gaps were a drag. Vicki read on.

. . . meanwhile, by using rewards and punishment in turn, the captain rendered even the upstanding members of the crew avaricious on the one hand and submissive on the other – two characteristics which, when they act in combination, inevitably encourage men to be brutal. I formed the impression that this was just what the captain desired.

Curiously enough, we set sail from our home port without taking on any cargo. With what, I wondered, did the captain propose to ply for trade? Nor did we put in at any other seaports, and the Storm Goddess's *spacious holds remained empty.*

We sailed south-east, but the captain kept our destination to himself. Although I thought at first that we were making for the west coast of Africa, I was undeceived of that notion when we put in at San Sebastián on the Canarian island of La Gomera. There we took on water and provisions in quantities that would have sufficed, not only for our forty-man crew, but for at least five times that number.

And then we sailed westward.

The captain still breathed no word of our destination, but it became clear that we were to sail back across the Atlantic Ocean with the trade wind, in accordance with the West Indiamen's old rule: south till the butter melts, then west.

Every sensible sea captain endeavours to complete an Atlantic passage as quickly as possible. Not so our new skipper. We carried only as much canvas as sufficed for an almost leisurely turn of speed, and we changed course at regular intervals. Moreover, the lookouts had been doubled. It was as if the captain meant to rendezvous with other ships. But with what ships, and to what end?

After only six days a brig hove into view. She turned out to be a courier ship of the Royal Navy, and she passed us at a considerable distance. After scrutinizing the brig, the captain shut his telescope and went below without a word.

The next vessel reported by the lookouts was a square-rigger, which rapidly overhauled us with all sails set. Having watched her for a while, the captain handed me his telescope and asked if anything about her struck me as odd.

I examined the ship but could not at first detect anything of note, save that her deck looked peculiarly dark. It was not until I focused the telescope with maximal clarity that I saw what the captain meant: the foredeck and amidships were swarming with dark-skinned figures.

The ship was a slaver.

She was one of those merchantmen whose cargo consists of blackamores being transported from Africa to the West Indies. This is a trade like any other, but far more profitable. Far more hazardous, too! It often happens that plague breaks out among the slaves and carries off the whole cargo, which has been purchased at a high price.

The slave ship, which soon drew level with us, must have been carrying some six hundred slaves. These are penned up below deck at night. By day, however, so as to preserve them in good health, they are permitted to enjoy the fresh air as naked as the day they were born. Every slave that perishes during a voyage betokens a financial loss.

The guarding and supervision of so large a number of slaves requires a sizeable crew, which the slaver clearly possessed. She hoisted her colours and we replied in kind, as etiquette prescribes when two ships meet on the high seas. 'May God and a fair wind be with you,' the captain muttered. 'You're too big a morsel for me.'

At the time, his meaning escaped me, but I was soon to be enlightened.

Barely a week later, the lookouts reported that another square-rigger was in sight. This time, we were the ones that approached from astern, for she was drifting along with her ill-set sails aflutter. The captain crowded on all sail, and we overhauled her within a few hours.

The ship's name was Fortuna. Her decks were entirely deserted, but on the foredeck was a large, windowless shack of the kind in which black women and their children are confined during the night.

The Fortuna, too, was a slaver.

Our captain hailed the ship with the aid of a loud-hailer, and it turned out that she was not devoid of life after all. A man emerged from the aft companionway and tottered over to a loud-hailer mounted on the bulwark. We blenched at the sight of him. It was apparent, even to the naked eye, that he had the Black Pox.

In a feeble voice, he stated that he was the boatswain of the Fortuna. Her captain and first mate had perished of the Black Pox, as had most of her crew. Only twelve men were still alive.

'What of your cargo?' called our captain. 'Have any of the slaves survived?'

Just then, another man emerged from the companionway. Less infirm than the boatswain, he introduced himself in a clear voice as the owner of the cargo. This did not surprise us, for it often happens that valuable cargo is accompanied by a representative of the owner, or even by the owner himself.

The owner informed us that the three hundred slaves on board were evidently immune to the Black Pox, as blackamores sometimes are, with the result that only a handful of them had died of thirst. But this availed him little, he said, for the cargo was lost come what may, there being insufficient room to accommodate the slaves aboard a merchantman such as the Storm Goddess.

Our captain instructed the two men to go to the stern cabin, taking their fellow sufferers with them, and remain there until permitted to come out. Obediently, the boatswain and the owner of the cargo disappeared aft. They realized, of course, that we had to take precautions against infection before we took them on board.

I asked our captain what was to become of the slaves, remarking that, contrary to their owner's belief, there was plenty of room for them aboard the unladen Storm Goddess. But the captain made no answer.

[Illegible]

Hmm. Vicki read on.

. . . our exceedingly arduous and unpleasant work was done at last, and the captain gave orders to cast off from the Fortuna. *I asked him whether he truly meant to condemn the poor souls aboard her to certain death. How dared I question his orders, he retorted, so I held my peace and did nothing.*

Had I, too, succumbed to the spirit of brutality?

We thereupon sailed west under a full spread of canvas and, without further incident, put in at . . .

[Illegible]

Feeling frustrated, Vicki turned the page.

The autumn was already far advanced by the time we neared our port of origin . . .

But what had happened in the meantime? Vicki shut the book and jumped up. The first mate had sealed the packet carefully, but the confounded sea water had seeped in all the same. She picked up the journal, then slammed it down on the desk.

'Vicki?' Her father was right outside the door. 'Vicki? What's the matter?'

'Er . . . ' She cleared her throat. 'Nothing.'

'You were making such funny noises.'

'Everything's fine.' Vicki glanced at her watch. Nearly

seven. Why wasn't he down in the kitchen? What was he doing up here?

'May I come in?'

'Sure.' She went to the door and unlocked it. But she'd forgotten the journal!

Her father had already come in. 'What are you reading?' he asked.

'Oh, nothing special.' Slowly and calmly, she walked back to the desk, turned around and leaned against it.

His chef's hat was now on straight – impeccably straight. He gave her a really searching stare. 'OK, maybe it's all for the best,' he said suddenly. 'It's your business, after all.' He paused. 'Listen, I hate to ask, but I need a favour.'

'What is it?' asked Vicki.

'Could you help serve the tables tonight?' Rather hurriedly, he added, 'Just for two or three hours. I've managed to hire a new waitress, but she can't start till tomorrow. Is that all right?'

'Fine,' she said. 'I'll be right down.'

'Thanks.' His eyes strayed past her to the bookshelf, then he turned and went out.

She locked the door again.

Quickly, she replaced the journal among her books. Another close call!

What had her father said? 'Maybe it's all for the best. It's your business, after all.'

It had sounded odd, somehow. Out of place, so to speak. But why?

Vicki shook her head.

Not now, she told herself. Your customers are waiting.

TWELVE

Phil was worried.

What was the harbour master doing here? The huge man was standing at the counter with a bald-headed, potato-nosed stranger, and both were digging into cod and chips, one of Phil's most popular dishes. The harbour master had a bottle of beer, and the bald-headed stranger was sipping a glass of water.

'Our Phil isn't the brightest individual,' the harbour master was saying, 'but his cod and chips are unbeatable.' And, to Phil, 'I should have paid you another visit a long time ago.'

Phil was really worried now.

The harbour master had come here to *eat*? Were they running a check on him? Was baldy from the council?

Phil wiped the counter vigorously, wondering whether he'd violated one of the innumerable hygiene regulations. He ran through them in his head, one by one, but came to no conclusion. He'd better be on his guard, that was all.

On the whole, though, he was feeling good. Business was brisk. The tables around his stand had been filled ever since lunchtime. A small generator was *put-put-putting* away behind the trailer, and he would soon be getting some outside lighting.

Why? Because some floodlights had been set up around the *Storm Goddess*.

Not to illuminate his fish and chip stand, of course, but so that the ship could be guarded more effectively. A start had been made with the camper van in which Phil's uncle and his sergeant had installed themselves. Neither of them seemed to expect the sea to come flooding back, nor did anyone else. Phil, who was slightly surprised by this, had taken the precaution of leaving the wheels on his trailer – at least for the time being.

'Know what, Phil?' said the harbour master. 'I'd like the same again. How about you?' he asked, turning to the stranger.

'Not for me,' said baldy. 'Maybe we could get down to business at last.'

'Calm down,' said the harbour master. 'First *you* were

dragging your feet, and now *I'm* taking my time.' The stranger flushed and muttered something unintelligible.

Vicki's new friend had been there that afternoon, the one with the little round glasses. He was nice, Phil decided. Peter had politely introduced himself and then his parents. *They* had *not* been pleasant, especially the mother, who'd only picked at her fish. They were measly little things, she said – not like the big fat ones you got in Spain. Unlike her, Peter's father – Hawaiian shirt and gold medallion on a chain around his neck – had praised Phil's fish to the skies. That was hot air, too. They were perfectly ordinary haddock of the kind that were caught off the coast here, and they were getting smaller every year because of the pollution.

'All right.' The harbour master had finished his meal. 'Let's go to the table round the back. We won't be disturbed there.' He and the bald-headed stranger disappeared around the corner.

Phil stepped back until all that separated him from them was the thin trailer wall.

'Why all the fuss?' he heard the stranger ask. 'Why drag me out to this crummy fish and chip stand?'

'Because I want to show the voters I'm not too proud to have a plate of Phil's finest in congenial company.' The harbour master chuckled. 'I've harnessed you to my

187

long-term election campaign, my friend.' Then he said curtly, 'Right, you wanted a word with me and here I am. What's up?'

Phil breathed a sigh of relief. Their meeting didn't concern him. He was about to resume his place behind the counter when he heard the stranger say, 'I insist you give me a free hand at last. I've got to search that ship.'

Phil stopped short. Was baldy one of the scientists?

'You said you reckoned the first mate's journal would tell you where the stuff is hidden. I thought you were planning to get it from the girl at the Seashell.'

'I not only planned to, I searched her room. There wasn't a sign of it.'

'That's great,' said the harbour master, and Phil could picture his scowling face. 'And you expect me to let you turn the *Storm Goddess* upside down just to find something that may only exist in your imagination?'

'You're down for a share of my "imaginary" gold, or had you forgotten?'

'No, I hadn't. A half share.'

'Are you mad? We agreed on a quarter.'

'I just upped it to half because you're being so uncooperative.' The harbour master fell silent. The stranger said nothing, either. Then the harbour master said, 'Well, is it a deal?'

'Have it your own way,' the stranger snarled. 'But I'll pay you back, believe me.'

'You don't scare me!'

'I want to get on to that ship tonight.'

'No, you don't. I'll decide when.' The harbour master paused. 'I hope you won't be stupid enough to go behind my back again.'

'You can't put me off much longer. That gold is mine, and I'm going to get it.'

'Be careful, my friend. My police officers are overworked and irritable. They might react violently – brutally, even – if they caught someone trying to sneak on board that ship without permission.'

It was absolutely soul-destroying.

Vicki had thought that helping serve tables at night would be a breeze. No families with small children, no ketchup on the tablecloths, no upset glasses of Coke.

Instead, it was: 'How old are you?' – 'Isn't it time you were in bed?' – 'Making a child wait at tables? Disgraceful!'

She'd trotted out her standard answer to questions about her age so often tonight – 'I look young for my age' – that she'd begun to believe it herself. That would have meant she looked younger than twelve. She probably looked like a nursery tot, the way she felt at present.

Never mind, though. Peter would turn up sometime –
and then, Eileen had promised, she could knock off.

When she actually caught sight of him in the doorway of
the restaurant, she gave such a delighted start, she almost
tipped a dish of lamb chops into a frozen-faced old woman's
lap.

But a big bunch of customers had come crowding into
the restaurant on Peter's heels. She looked enquiringly at
Eileen, who shook her head.

'Here, take my key,' she told Peter. 'I'm sorry, I can't
come just yet.'

'No problem,' he said with a smile. 'After all, I've got
some reading to do up there.'

Less than an hour later, the Seashell began to empty
quite quickly, and Vicki was free to go.

Up in her bedroom, she found Peter staring peevishly out
of the window with the first mate's journal lying open on
the desk. 'Another stupid "Illegible"!' he said. 'I'd give
anything to know how that business with the slave ship
turned out.'

Vicki glanced at the book. He'd read precisely as far as
she had.

'By the way,' he said, his face brightening, 'after spending
the afternoon with my parents, they said I could stay out
late. It was a good investment.'

Vicki laughed.

'I could probably even sleep over again,' he suggested.

She was about to say 'Good,' when her mobile rang. 'Yes?'

'Rose here. I have to see you tonight. Peter, too, preferably. Can you make it?'

'Sure, right away? At the newspaper office?'

'No, not there. Do you know the aquarium?'

'Of course. Will it still be open?'

'Yes. See you there in fifteen minutes.'

One visit to the aquarium was enough to last a lifetime. Vicki had been there on a school outing at the age of nine. She remembered trailing miserably past some weed-encrusted plate-glass windows behind which teemed all manner of hideous sea creatures whose presence there was attributable solely to the fact that nobody fancied eating them.

There was a poster outside the entrance. It proclaimed: *Monsters of the Deep! See the Man-eating Sharks!*

'Hey,' said Peter, pointing to it, 'that sounds promising.'

Vicki said nothing. He would see soon enough that the sharks were the length of a man's arm and about as dangerous to humans as sardines.

'Hi, Vicki,' said the lady at the cash desk. She was one of

the two women who gave the Seashell Restaurant a thorough cleaning once a week. 'I was just going to close for the night.'

'Can I quickly show my friend the sharks?'

'Be my guest. The young lady from the newspaper is still inside. Go right in.'

Rose was waiting beside the tank containing the sharks. The three so-called sea monsters, all of which had grown a bit since Vicki's last visit, were swimming restlessly in a circle. 'Pathetic, isn't it?' said Rose. 'They remind me of caged tigers.'

'Sharks don't have any air bladders,' said Peter. 'They have to keep moving or they'll sink to the bottom.'

'You don't say!' Rose was clearly impressed.

Vicki was less so. She'd also paid attention in science lessons.

'They aren't man-eaters, of course.' Peter had gone right up to the glass. 'All the same, I wouldn't like them to take a bite out of me.'

He was so right – they were far too small to be man-eaters. 'Why didn't we meet at the newspaper office?' Vicki asked Rose.

'Because the walls there have ears, and I don't want anything to leak out before I've assembled all the evidence.'

'Evidence? Of what?'

'First things first.' Rose looked around. She, Vicki and Peter were alone in the aquarium. No one was looking at them except the three tirelessly circling sharks. 'I did some research this afternoon. I wanted to find out exactly who or what Belper is. But then I thought: why not first take a look under "Storm Goddess" in the public records. That wasn't such a good idea. All I found was a kind of memorandum stating that the first mate's journal had been washed ashore and that your family, Vicki, has a printed copy. I already knew that. But then I had a flash of inspiration. I looked under a completely different keyword, and I hit the jackpot!' Rose surveyed them triumphantly.

'What keyword?' asked Vicki.

'I won't tell you that yet, but here's the jackpot.' Rose produced several sheets of paper from her shoulder bag.

'These are copies of something written in pen and ink,' said Peter. 'In that old-fashioned script, but I can't read it. Only the numerals 1-7-7-3. Is that the date?'

Rose nodded. 'This is a record of the proceedings of a maritime court held in the spring of 1773.' She proceeded to read aloud: '"Enquiries relating to the captain of the *Storm Goddess*."'

'You mean you can read that old writing?' Peter was impressed.

So was Vicki, actually, but she didn't think Peter needed to smile so broadly at Rose. Very briskly, she said, 'So the maritime court investigated the captain. Why?'

Rose looked at the document. '"The said enquiries,"' she read aloud, '"established beyond doubt that the above-named captain had taken possession of the *Fortuna*'s cargo by illicit means."'

Vicki and Peter exchanged a look.

'He took the slaves on board the *Storm Goddess*,' said Vicki.

'But in that case, who were the "poor souls"?' Peter adjusted his glasses. 'The first mate asked the captain if he . . . what did it say? He asked "whether he truly meant to condemn the poor souls aboard her to certain death." That's what it says in the journal, but you can't tell who he's talking about.' He stared at Rose. 'You mean . . . ?'

Rose nodded. 'Yes, the "poor souls" were the members of the crew who hadn't yet died of the Black Pox. The captain left them behind on the *Fortuna*. He condemned them to death.' She consulted the papers again. '"The slaves are estimated to have numbered approximately three hundred,"' she read out. '"The proceeds of their sale, based on an average price of five doubloons per slave—"'

'Came to fifteen hundred doubloons!' Vicki exclaimed.

'Now we know where the captain got his gold – from the slaves he sold!'

'Yes,' said Rose, 'he stole them and converted them into cash. That's why he left the men from the *Fortuna* behind. He wanted them out of the way.'

'But . . . ' Peter shook his head. 'If they were all dead, how did the court find out about it?'

'Good question,' said Rose, smiling at Peter – for no good reason, thought Vicki. 'The thing is, they weren't all dead. One of them survived and was rescued by a passing merchantman. This lone survivor was, wait for it, the slave owner!'

Peter smiled back at her; a little too friendly, thought Vicki. 'And he set the enquiry in motion,' he said.

'But it came to nothing,' Vicki said quickly, before all this smiling got out of hand, 'because the *Storm Goddess* had disappeared. But, Rose, we still don't know how Belper got to know about the gold on board the *Storm Goddess*.'

'Another good question,' said Rose, smiling at *her* this time, although she hadn't asked a question at all. 'But the answer is obvious once you know what the slave owner's name was.' She paused. 'I searched the records using the man's name as a keyword. It was—'

'Belper!' cried Vicki.

Rose nodded. 'Right.'

'That's unbelievable!' Vicki said in an awestruck voice.

Peter nodded, looking equally amazed.

After a while, Vicki said, 'Well, that explains everything. You've got all the evidence we need.'

But Rose shook her head. 'No, not yet. The most important piece of evidence is still missing.'

'What's that?'

'Proof that Belper and the harbour master are in this together.'

Just then Vicki's mobile rang. 'Hello?'

'Hi there, Vicki, it's Phil here. I've got a question for you: who's the girl at the Seashell?'

'Me, I guess.'

'In that case, a bald-headed man searched your room.'

'How do *you* know?'

'I would have called you earlier, but I got busy. Anyway, I overheard this baldy telling the harbour master about it.'

'You actually overheard him?' Vicki reacted swiftly. 'Look, Phil, would you mind telling Rose Redd about this? Right now?'

'The reporter, you mean? If you think I should.'

'Yes, I think you should.' Vicki passed the phone to Rose. 'It's Phil from the fish and chip stand,' she said. And, when Rose gave an enquiring shrug, she added, 'He's got the proof.'

*   *   *

It was all settled.

They would make another attempt to get on board the *Storm Goddess* that very night.

Having quickly briefed Vicki and Peter on what Phil had told her, Rose hurried off to plan her next move. Through their plate-glass window the three so-called man-eaters paused to watch her go, then noticed they were sinking and resumed their restless circling.

There was no time to lose, that was clear. If Belper was going to search the *Storm Goddess*, with or without the harbour master's backing, he would have to do so by night. And if Vicki and Peter were to stand any chance at all, they would also have to operate under cover of darkness.

'What about the cops in the camper van?' said Peter. 'Not to mention those floodlights? It'll be like daylight out there.'

Vicki nodded. 'I've got an idea, though. All we need is a bit of,' – she looked at Peter – 'no, a bit's no good. We're going to need a *lot* of luck. A *whole* lot of luck.'

'If not more,' said Peter. 'More than anybody's entitled to.' He returned Vicki's gaze. 'Do you really *have* to do this?'

'I do,' she said.

Peter's face broke into a sudden smile. 'Then, as I said once before, I'm coming with you.'

Vicki smiled back at him. It was unimaginable, the idea of coping with the secret of the Storm Goddess on her own, and it hadn't occurred to her only 'once before'. She'd thought of it – no, she'd sensed it – every minute of the day.

'To start with,' she said, 'maybe we'll only need a *little* luck.' She took out her mobile and keyed in a number. 'Hi, Phil. Are you still out at the ship?'

THIRTEEN

The sky had clouded over by the time Vicki and Peter sneaked out of the house. Intermittent gusts of wind kept blowing the clouds apart, bathing the road along the quay in brilliant moonlight. Only briefly, though, and the ensuing darkness seemed twice as dark.

Vicki was feeling slightly bemused. She shook her head to clear it.

She'd been through all this before!

Suddenly she felt trapped in a time warp – doomed to do the same thing over and over again for ever more. The dazed sensation persisted as she and Peter approached the railings.

When they reached them, however, her feeling of déjà vu vanished in a flash, for she'd never before seen the sight that met her eyes, not the way it looked now.

The bay stretched away in front of her like a turbulent sea, alternately flooded with moonlight and plunged in gloom. And in the midst of that turbulent sea, as if stranded on an island, lay the floodlit *Storm Goddess*. She lay there becalmed and motionless – indeed, Vicki had the impression that her sails were hanging limp from the yards despite the flurries of wind.

The *Storm Goddess* lay there as if she – no, as if *someone* – were saying, *Here I am, waiting for you*. It wasn't just an invitation presented by the rope ladder dangling down the ship's side. It was a plea from the first mate.

Vicki pictured him gazing at her gravely, intently, and all at once she understood. His was no request; he was entrusting her with a mission. A mission she must carry out at all costs. The first mate's gaze was a command. A command she had to obey. And when she realized she had no choice, she felt scared. Terribly scared. Almost panic-stricken, in fact.

She looked at Peter, who was standing silently beside her. Why didn't he say something? 'We didn't need our torches,' she said. 'It's very light by the ship.'

'What if we have to go below deck? It'll be pitch-dark down there.'

Descend into the spooky bowels of the *Storm Goddess*?

Vicki hadn't thought of that. Peter had, but he was keeping his cool in spite of his doubts as to whether the whole operation was necessary.

They made their way down the slipway to the beach and set off across the mud flats towards the *Storm Goddess*. Vicki's panic subsided.

Before long, she could make out some details: the light in the windows of the camper van – Inspector Grogan was on duty tonight, according to Phil – and the glow from the fish and chip stand. 'An excuse for staying out here late?' Phil had said. 'No problem. I'll give my place another thorough spring-cleaning. Public health regulations, et cetera. Between you and me, it'll take hours.'

They had agreed that Vicki and Peter would get to the *Storm Goddess* by half past twelve. Exactly what Phil would do then, they didn't know. 'I'll think of something,' he'd told them. 'But why do you want to get on board the ship?'

'I have to, Phil. I can't tell you why because I don't know myself, but I have to.'

'OK,' Phil said. 'Don't worry, I won't let you down.'

She wasn't worried where Phil was concerned. What worried her as she trudged toward the *Storm Goddess* with Peter at her side was the moonlight, which kept flooding the bay. What if Grogan spotted them crossing the mud flats?

But then, as if the moon had read her thoughts, it veiled itself in cloud. The sky was completely overcast now; she couldn't see a single star, and the wind seemed to have gone to sleep.

It was unlikely that Grogan would hear them. Phil had mentioned that a generator had been installed beside the ship to power the floodlights. She could already hear its distant hum.

They made a detour to the right to keep the trailer between them and the camper van. That would hide them from view for the last two or three hundred metres, which were brightly lit by the floodlights.

The *Storm Goddess* loomed up ahead.

And hanging from the bulwark amidships was the rope ladder.

They crept up to the trailer.

Phil had positioned it so that the ship was visible from the counter. Vicki and Peter made for the door at the rear, keeping low. The generator beside the ship wasn't as loud as Vicki had expected, and Phil's little generator was quieter still.

She tapped on the door.

It opened a crack, and Phil put his head out. 'Right,' he said, 'this is it. As soon as I'm inside that camper van, climb aboard like greased lightning. For now, hide round the corner.' He withdrew his head and shut the door.

'What's he up to?' asked Peter as they followed Phil's directions.

Vicki shrugged. 'Search me.'

At that moment a scream rang out from inside the trailer – a loud and rather bloodcurdling scream. The door burst open and Phil came dashing out. He was clutching his left hand with his right and wailing, 'My hand! My hand!' He ran over to the gate in the fence, still crying, 'My hand! My hand!'

Inspector Grogan emerged from the police trailer. 'What's up?' he called. 'What's the matter with you?'

But Phil just went on. 'My hand! My hand!'

Grogan hurried over to the gate and opened it. 'What have you done?'

'I was cleaning my carving knife,' said Phil, 'and I cut myself! Ouch! It hurts!'

'Why can't you be more careful?' Grogan said testily. 'All right, come in.' He towed Phil over to the camper van and disappeared inside with him. 'Sharp knives need handling with care, you imbecile,' Vicki and Peter heard before the door closed, muffling Phil's wails and Grogan's indignant voice.

'Great,' said Peter, 'let's go.'

They sprinted through the gate, which Grogan hadn't

bothered to close, and over to the rope ladder.

Vicki put her foot on the bottom rung, then hesitated. Something seemed to be holding her back, but what?

Phil's muffled wails and Grogan's grumbles were still issuing from the camper van.

Then she knew what was holding her back: she hadn't the faintest idea what was waiting for her on board the *Storm Goddess*. What if it was something that made a lot of noise? If so, Grogan would climb on board immediately.

No, now wasn't the time. She and Peter had arranged things perfectly with Phil. Or almost perfectly, because they'd overlooked this one possibility. I promise I'll come on board, Vicki thought, but I can't come now.

And then she heard voices.

They were coming from the stern. She looked at Peter.

'I can hear them too,' he whispered. 'Shall we get closer?' Vicki nodded, and they hurried along the side to the stern.

It was the two men they'd heard last night.

And, as before, their subdued but angry voices were coming from the captain's cabin. Vicki caught little of what they were saying at first, but she could distinguish the captain's voice from the first mate's.

Suddenly the captain roared, 'Where are they, those doubloons? You had no right to take them, you and your cronies. Where have you hidden them?!'

'I won't tell you!' the first mate shouted back. 'That gold isn't rightfully ours. It'll be the ruin of us!'

The two men had uttered the same words last night, Vicki felt certain, but somehow they'd sounded different. She took a moment to grasp what the difference was. The words were identical, but not in emphasis and volume. The captain had shouted much louder last night, whereas now it was the first mate whose voice sounded loud and piercing. It was as if two actors had been made to repeat their lines, but in another way.

'For the last time,' cried the captain, 'where are those doubloons?!'

'You can search the ship from stem to stern!' the first mate retorted. 'You'll never find them!'

A chair scraped on the deck.

'Come back here!' yelled the man with the booming voice. A door slammed. 'Come back, you dog!' There was a clatter, then the door slammed again.

The sounds were now coming from overhead. More doors slammed, footsteps raced across the deck. Then came a gunshot.

Although Vicki had been expecting the shot, it gave her a terrible fright.

'Come on, men, to arms!' bellowed the captain. 'Show these cowardly mutineers! Save your gold!'

'On deck, all who fear God and the law!' shouted the first mate. 'Show these lawbreakers! Save the ship!'

As before, the deck abruptly resounded to a multitude of hurrying footsteps. A babble of voices arose, mingled with the dull thud of blows and the clash of steel on steel.

Then came the second gunshot followed by the single cry. Again, it sounded so agonized and prolonged that Vicki felt like putting her hands over her ears.

Unexpectedly, silence fell.

All that could be heard was the muffled hum of the generators.

And then came a clatter.

It didn't come from up on deck or from inside the ship. It came from outside. Cautiously, Vicki and Peter moved leftward until they could look along the port side.

Inspector Grogan had propped an aluminium ladder beside the rope ladder and was halfway up it. He was climbing slowly, holding on with his left hand alone. Clutched in his right hand was a police revolver.

He reached the top, climbed over the bulwark to the deck, and disappeared from view. Vicki and Peter listened hard. For a while they heard nothing, then his footsteps crossing the deck.

All at once he came to a halt.

Another silence followed.

Then they heard him break into a run. Having scrambled back over the bulwark and on to the ladder with surprising agility – his revolver was back in its holster – Grogan climbed down in a tearing hurry. He dashed over to the camper van and disappeared inside.

The door soon opened, and Phil emerged with a bandage around his left hand. Excitedly, he gestured up at the *Storm Goddess*.

Vicki and Peter looked at each other.

It was Vicki who hesitated. 'Do you think we should?'

'If we don't, we'll never know what Grogan saw.'

'OK, let's go.'

They ran to the aluminium ladder and climbed up it fast, Vicki in the lead, then lowered themselves to the deck.

The first thing Vicki noticed was its cleanliness. For some reason she had assumed that the *Storm Goddess* would be in a dirty, disorderly state, but the deck was perfectly shipshape and as clean as a house-proud housekeeper's kitchen floor.

And then, on the planks beside the forward companion-way, Vicki caught sight of a dark patch.

It was around a metre across, and it reflected the light. It was a glistening pool of something.

She went closer. The pool *was* dark – dark *red*.

'My God,' Peter whispered behind her, 'it's blood.'

She stood and stared at it. It could also be red paint, she thought. But it *was* blood. What did the first mate expect of her? Here she was, standing on the *Storm Goddess's* scrubbed deck, summoned here and quite prepared to do whatever was expected of her . . . but . . . real blood?! And so *much* of it . . . a whole bucketful . . . could someone really have lost that much? Vicki couldn't imagine it . . . she was stupefied.

What was that? A sound had penetrated her thoughts.

'A car's coming!' Peter hissed behind her. 'It must be the police.'

Her stupefaction vanished in an instant. 'Come on, let's get off!'

They dashed to the side. And there, outside the camper van, stood Grogan. He was looking in the direction of the approaching vehicle's headlights, his back to the ship.

'Come on, down the ladder,' Vicki whispered.

'What if he turns round?' Peter whispered back. 'We'd better hide on board.'

'But they'll search the ship.'

'You're right. Let's go!'

They climbed quickly down the aluminium ladder. Vicki didn't even glance in Grogan's direction; she would know soon enough if he'd spotted her. She reached the ground and flitted along the side to the stern with Peter close behind her. 'We were lucky.'

Peter merely nodded. After a while, he said, 'All that blood—' He broke off, staring into space, then looked at Vicki. 'Someone really *is* waiting for you up there.'

'I know,' was all she said.

They listened in silence to the hum of the approaching police car. The siren wasn't blaring. The harbour master doesn't want to attract attention, Vicki told herself.

She said aloud, 'I wonder what the harbour master will dream up this time.' And, when Peter looked at her enquiringly, she said, 'Well, the blood can't very well have come from a pirate film.'

The car pulled up. Vicki peeked around the corner. The harbour master jumped out and strode through the gate in the fence, followed by Sergeant Willis. 'Well, come on,' he snapped at Grogan. 'Show me your nice surprise.'

Grogan led the way to the ladder and climbed aboard, followed by the harbour master and Willis.

'Hmm,' Vicki heard the harbour master say. 'This blood looks pretty fresh. Are you sure there was no one on board, Inspector?'

'Absolutely, sir. I had the ship under constant surveillance.'

'So nobody knows about the blood aside from you, me, and the sergeant?'

'That's correct.'

'How about that nephew of yours? What's he doing here at this hour?'

'His trailer needed a thorough spring-cleaning.'

'Well, does he know about this?'

'Er, I—'

'Does he or doesn't he?'

'He doesn't, sir,' Grogan said smartly. 'He was in his trailer the whole time.'

'Good.' The harbour master seemed to be deliberating. 'If this gets into the papers, we can forget the *Storm Goddess* as a tourist attraction. If anyone asks about the noise, Inspector, we'll issue the same explanation that acoustics expert gave.'

'But what about the blood, harbour master?'

The harbour master remained silent for quite a while. Then Vicki and Peter heard him say, 'What I'm going to tell you now is thoroughly illegal. If this leaks out, we'll be out of a job, all three of us.' He paused. 'The only difference being that you two will be sitting on the quay with a notice saying *Unemployed* and a cardboard cup full of change, whereas I'll finally be able to take all those holidays I've never managed to fit in before. Get the picture?'

'Perfectly, sir.'

'Glad to hear it. Now, listen closely: get rid of that blood, OK?'

'Yes, sir. How?'

'How? By swabbing the deck, of course. You can get hold of a bucket and some water, can't you?'

'Certainly we can, sir.'

'Good. And search the ship from top to bottom. If you find anything suspicious, get rid of that, too. Do I make myself clear?'

'Absolutely, sir.'

The harbour master climbed back down the ladder, followed by Grogan and Willis. The sergeant resumed his place behind the wheel of the police car, the harbour master got into the passenger seat, and they zoomed off across the mud flats.

Grogan stood staring after them. Then he turned and looked up at the bow of the ship.

Phil came and stood beside him.

'Curse this confounded hulk!' Grogan growled. 'I knew it meant trouble from the start.'

'Why?' asked Phil.

'A figurehead without a head? Any fool knows that brings bad luck.'

FOURTEEN

The autumn was already far advanced by the time we neared our port of origin.

I truly cherished the hope, even then, that this voyage would have a happy ending. How could I have been so blind? How could I have forgotten the old saying that one wrong breeds another? How could I have believed that ill-gotten gold would redound to our advantage?

I was soon taught otherwise, and in terrible fashion, by the cruel injustice done to the young sailor known as Simple Simon. His corpse still hangs from the main yardarm, from which, on the captain's orders, it may not be taken down. 'Lookee here,' it seems to say. 'A like fate awaits all who break their oath!' We are all sworn never to disclose the source of the gold.

I shall have to lay this journal aside ere long. The captain put on every stitch of canvas after the terrible occurrence, but he will soon, no doubt, be compelled to hoist storm-sails, for the wind appears to be getting up. No, it isn't the wind . . . I hear a strange roaring sound . . . .What can it be? I . . .

At least half an hour has passed since I penned the above – half an hour in which our fate may have been sealed.

The aforesaid roaring sound was succeeded by a mighty jolt that shook the entire vessel. The deck was ankle-deep in water, streams of which poured from the scuppers.

A single, mast-high wave had overtaken the Storm Goddess. Although towering waves of this kind are encountered in the Pacific Ocean, I had not known that they can also occur in these latitudes. Be that as it may, the wave caused no damage to the ship herself. All the hatch covers over the companionways had been battened down, God be praised, nor did any of the crew go overboard. All that was carried away and washed overboard from the afterdeck, never to be seen again, was the head of our figurehead.

The ship's carpenter swore that he had lashed the head down securely, but all his asseverations to that effect and the captain's fury were to no avail. The worst had happened: the Storm Goddess had been abandoned by her protectress.

The captain promptly called the crew together and harangued them. We were nearing our home port, he reminded them, so the likelihood of another mishap was extremely small. Furthermore, he announced that he would shortly be sharing out the gold.

This might possibly have reassured the men, had he not gone on to say and do something that may have achieved the opposite effect – certainly, unless I am much mistaken, where some of the crew are concerned.

The captain said he knew that many sailors believed the presence of a hanged man on board to be unlucky. For that reason, he proposed to have Simple Simon cut down and committed to the deep as custom and piety prescribed, which he immediately did.

This, I believe, made it clear to those of the crew who had not been altogether brutalized that—

A knock at my cabin door.

We are done for!

We are all accursed and done for, that is now plain to see.

I must quell my agitation. Perhaps there is still a way out, although I have little hope of it. We must keep calm now. Calm.

It was barely an hour ago when there came a knock at the door of my cabin, and there stood without some representatives of the crew. More precisely, a delegation drawn from the Gertrude's former crew and led by the boatswain.

It was as I had supposed. These men, who had remained upright in their innermost hearts, had become aware of the crime they had committed (and I with them!) in consenting to hang Simple Simon. Now that the Storm Goddess *had been abandoned by her figurehead*, they had concluded that, for honest men, only one choice remained: to forgo their share of the gold and quit the ship. In short, I was requested to prevail upon the captain to permit the Gertrude's former hands (half of the Storm Goddess's crew) to depart.

Would I, they asked, act as their spokesman?

I was only too willing to do so, for I shared their opinion in all respects, so I went to see the captain. To my surprise, he agreed forthwith, doubtless believing that he could complete the remainder of the voyage with a diminished crew. Above all, he would now have to share the gold with only half as many men. He could rest assured that none of us would report its existence to the authorities, every one of us being bound to silence by our complicity in the hanging of that poor lad.

The captain let us have one of the two lifeboats (each of them large enough to accommodate half the ship's company), and we lowered away. Down the ladder we went, one by one, to the accompaniment of jeers and catcalls from those who preferred to remain aboard the Storm Goddess.

And then, just as we were casting off, a second wave bore down on us, powerful enough to capsize our boat and sink it. By some miracle, we all managed to scramble up the ladder and get back on board. But we are done for notwithstanding.

The Storm Goddess *has been forsaken by her protectress*,

and we are all, without exception, condemned to remain aboard her – as men accursed.

Every sailor knows the legend of the 'Ghost Ship', of the crew whose dreadful acts have condemned them to eternal . . . no! My pen balks at completing this sentence! The very thought is too terrible to contemplate.

There must be some means of escape, but how?

The gold! That is the root of all our misfortune. It has . . .

[Illegible]

. . . and I shall keep this a secret for as long as I am able. This course of action, if any, may spell our salvation. But I must satisfy myself once more of the loyalty of the Gertrude's original crew, for there is every chance that it will come to a fight – a fight between those who are greedy for gold and those who have rediscovered their fear of God and the law.

So as not to dishearten the latter, I shall tell them that it is our duty to preserve the ship from disaster. I am far from confident, but I hope and pray that we shall be able to save our souls, if nothing else.

If not – no, it must not happen. That would be terrible, unthinkable!

The wind is rising. The storm that has been brewing for a considerable time is about to break.

I shall now end this journal. I intend to seal it up in a water-proof packet and commit it to the waves. Perhaps it will be *washed ashore and found.*

And, should we be doomed to the Terrible, the Unthinkable, there may come a day, if it please Almighty God, when my journal will become our anchor on this side of Eternity.

If not, may it bear witness, for the edification of posterity, to what occurred aboard the Storm Goddess.

May God have mercy on our souls.

FIFTEEN

It was half past ten, and Vicki was having a late breakfast in the Seashell. She'd made herself a plate of bacon and eggs and a steaming mug of hot chocolate. After that, if she still had room, there were plenty of crusty rolls and a basketful of little jars of jam to choose from. Her bacon and eggs were getting cold. If Peter didn't appear soon, she would start without him.

He was still upstairs in the guest room, reading the first mate's journal.

Which Vicki had really meant to finish reading herself.

She'd woken up just after ten, recalled the night's events, and taken the journal from her bookshelf. What had happened on board the *Storm Goddess* immediately before the fight broke out? She was eager to know that – right away, before breakfast. She'd thumbed through the little book in search of the place where she'd stopped reading. And where Peter had stopped reading too.

Just as she started to read, her mobile rang.

'Hello?'

'Morning, Vicki, it's me.'

'Peter! Where are you? I mean, where are you calling from?'

'The guest room. I'm not dressed yet, and I don't want to go out into the hall in my pyjamas. I might give your father or Eileen a heart attack.'

Vicki laughed. 'They don't frighten easily. Besides, they're out shopping at this hour.'

'Really? In that case can I come and get it myself? The journal, I mean. I was going to ask you to bring it to me. I wanted to finish reading it before breakfast.'

'But I've just started reading it.'

'Oh,' said Peter.

She'd always read it first, Vicki thought. Now it was Peter's turn. 'No problem, I'll bring it to you.'

She quickly got dressed, picked up the book, walked down the corridor to his room, and knocked.

The door opened, and Peter's head appeared. His hair was as tousled as a wire-haired terrier's fur, and he blinked at her through his glasses, which he carefully adjusted with his forefinger. Vicki passed him the book and made her way down to the restaurant.

Vicki was happy. Not just because Peter was here, but because she'd had the idea of letting him read the journal first.

But she really couldn't wait any longer. She forked up some bacon and egg and put it to her mouth.

At that moment, Peter appeared in the doorway.

He was still in his pyjamas and just as tousle-headed as before, but he wasn't blinking any more. His eyes were wide and staring. Slowly, holding up the journal, he said, 'I just realized something.'

He came over and sat down, depositing the book on the table. 'It occurred to me just as I finished reading.'

'Well?'

'There's a story I read once. A ghost story.' He looked at Vicki. 'I think I know what's going on aboard the *Storm Goddess*.'

'What's going on? How do you mean?'

'First I'll tell you the story. It's about a young merchant who goes on a sea voyage with his manservant. Their ship sinks, but they cling to a hatch cover until a mysterious sailing ship appears. They manage to climb aboard, but once on deck they get a terrible fright.'

'How come?'

'Because the deck is littered with dead bodies, one of which is pinned to the mast with a nail through its skull.'

'Ugh, how gruesome.' Vicki gave a little shudder. 'But what does this have to do with the Storm Goddess?'

'I'm coming to that. So they get a fright, but then they search the ship. Not a living soul to be seen, only dead bodies. Oh well, they think, anything's better than drowning, so they make themselves at home in the captain's cabin.' Peter paused. Then he said, 'That night it happens.'

'What does?'

'Two men suddenly materialize. They're sitting at the captain's table, yelling at each other, and one of them has a nail through his skull. It's the dead man who was pinned to the mast.'

Vicki said nothing. She wondered at first what this had to do with the Storm Goddess, but she was beginning to have a vague idea.

'Then the two sailors dash outside,' Peter went on, 'and pandemonium breaks out on deck. There's a fight in progress up there, no doubt about it. The members of the crew are fighting one another. But then everything goes quiet.' Peter fell silent for a moment. 'And the next morning?' he went on. 'What do you think the deck looks like the next morning?'

'Like . . .' Vicki gulped. 'Like it did the day before?'

'Exactly. The dead bodies are lying where they were, and the man is nailed to the mast.' Peter looked at her. 'Guess what happens the next night?'

'The two men start yelling at each other again, and the crew—'

'That's right, another fight breaks out.'

Vicki hesitated. 'You mean . . . ?'

Peter nodded. 'The crew is doomed to sail the seas and fight their last fight for eternity. Because there's a curse on them.'

'Why?'

'They committed a terrible crime.'

A crime! Vicki stared into space. After a while she said, 'The crew of the *Storm Goddess* hanged Simple Simon.' She looked at Peter. 'That laid a curse on *them*.'

'Yes, they're doomed to fight their last fight over and over again. The fight between the captain's men and the first mate's.'

Vicki suddenly felt as dizzy as if she'd just had a ride on a giant roller coaster. It can't be true, she thought. A ghost ship out in the bay, manned by a doomed crew . . . the first mate, who had appeared to her in the flesh . . . had it all been a dream, or was she out of her mind?

She looked across the table at Peter, who was still sitting

222

there in his pyjamas, hair tousled, fiddling with his glasses. Peter, who wanted to be a scientist. Scientists only believe in things for which there are rational explanations, yet there he sat, convinced that the crew of the *Storm Goddess* was under a curse – that they were doomed to repeat their last fight again and again. A fight they'd first fought two hundred and thirty years ago . . .

'There's something I don't understand,' she said. 'According to you, the crew of the *Storm Goddess* has to keep on fighting, over and over, but *when* do they fight? They've only fought twice since they appeared in the bay—' She broke off. Then, looking dumbfounded, she said, 'It was only when *we* wanted to go aboard.'

Peter shook his head. 'No, only when *you* did.'

Of course. The first mate was waiting for *her* out there, but what did he want her for? He had summoned her on board, that was clear, but what then? What would happen?

Why should she go on to the ship?

She looked across the table again. Peter was looking at her intently.

As if he knew the answer.

And instantly she knew it, too.

The first mate and the *Storm Goddess*'s crew wanted her to lift the curse!

For two hundred and thirty years they had been

condemned to sail the seas and repeat their last fight ad infinitum, but her discovery of the picture of the hanged man had suddenly presented them with a chance of escaping the curse. All that had happened since then: the sea's disappearance, the ship's appearance, had been meant to pave the way for her to go aboard.

Vicki hesitated. Then she asked, 'How did the story of the ghost ship end?'

'The curse was lifted.'

She was tempted to ask how, but she didn't. It didn't matter how the curse was lifted in Peter's story. The story of the *Storm Goddess* was different, and would end in a different way.

But how in the world were she and Peter going to slip past the police and escape detection a second time?

Vicki's stomach tied itself in knots as she realized that this was impossible. It simply couldn't be done. It was unthinkable.

But the idea of abandoning the first mate and the crew of the *Storm Goddess* to their fate was even more unthinkable.

She *had* to get on board that ship – tonight.

Peter turned pale when it became clear that they couldn't afford to spend time on preparations. They had to make another attempt tonight, no matter what.

It was Rose who had put them on the spot.

Rose, of all people, whom they'd intended to ask if she could think of a way for them to get aboard the *Storm Goddess* unobserved.

Vicki had called her from the phone on the serving counter and pressed the speakerphone button so Peter could listen in. 'We need your advice. Could we meet up? Today?'

'Not today, I'm afraid. I'm out of town – just left. I'd much rather finish my article exposing that unsavoury pair, but my editor wants me to find the place where the sound of pirates fighting came from.'

'You can save yourself the trouble,' said Vicki.

'Why? Do you know where it is?'

'No, because it doesn't ex—' Vicki broke off. Rose knew nothing about last night's pool of blood, which proved that the din of battle had come from the *Storm Goddess* herself, not from any pirate film. She itched to tell Rose the truth, but what if the reporter wrote about it? Or even hinted at it? The harbour master would assume that one of the policemen had blabbed – or both of them. He might even suspect Phil.

She needed time to think it over and discuss it with Peter.

'Well?' said Rose. 'What about this place?'

Vicki looked at Peter.

'Nothing. We don't know where it is.'

'Pity. In that case, my article on Belper and the harbour master will have to wait till this evening.'

'What are you planning to write about them?' Vicki asked.

'Can you keep it to yourselves?'

'Scouts' honour.'

'OK. Of course I won't reveal who told me they intend to split the gold fifty-fifty.'

'Certainly not,' said Vicki. That would have landed Phil in deep trouble.

'Besides, they'd deny it point-blank. However, I can still put a spoke in their wheel. It'll be enough if I stick to the facts I *can* prove. I'll say the captain of the *Storm Goddess* sold the *Fortuna*'s slaves for fifteen hundred gold doubloons, and that they must still be hidden somewhere on board. If I make it clear that those two scumbags know of the gold's existence, any reader will put two and two together. It'll knock them sideways, you wait and see!'

'But what good will it do?' asked Peter.

'Well, the authorities will search the ship very thoroughly. If the gold turns up, well and good. If not, it'll mean there isn't any on board after all. Either way, Belper and the harbour master will be scuppered. If the gold's found they won't see a penny of it; if it's not they'll have been plotting for nothing.' Rose paused. 'By the way, I'm convinced the gold exists.'

'You'll be even more convinced when you've read the first mate's journal,' said Peter.

'So when do I get to see it?'

'As soon as you like. We're just finishing it,' said Vicki.

'Today is no good, but I want to publish my scoop as soon as possible.' Rose paused again. She seemed to be deliberating. Then she said, 'I think I should be able to make tomorrow morning's edition.' And that was when Peter turned pale.

'What?' Vicki almost shouted the word. 'Tomorrow?' She pulled herself together. 'Can't you wait another day or two?'

'Why?'

'Because . . . because . . . '

'Give me one good reason why I should wait.'

'It's to do with what we wanted to discuss with you.'

Vicki was faced with a split-second decision. Should she tell Rose about the pool of blood? She did some mental arithmetic. So far, only six people knew about it. All at once she realized that the harbour master, the two policemen, and Phil had got to know about it by accident, so to speak. It had really been a message meant for her and

Peter. For the two of them, no one else. 'No,' Vicki said, 'I can't tell you over the phone.'

'Then it'll have to wait till tomorrow. Bye for now.' And the line went dead.

'Wait till tomorrow?' Vicki repeated.

Peter ran his fingers through his tousled hair. 'I wish it was tomorrow now.'

Phil's left thumb was thickly bandaged.

'What happened?' Vicki asked, pointing to it.

'I cut myself, remember?'

She stared at him. 'You did *what*? You mean to say you actually—'

'Cut myself? Of course, what did you expect? My uncle isn't *that* stupid. I couldn't go bleating to him with nothing to show for it.'

'You cut yourself *deliberately*?' Peter was equally flabbergasted. 'With a knife?'

'It was all I had handy.' Phil grinned.

'Phil, that was great of you,' said Vicki, and Peter nodded. 'Really great.'

'Yes, right, thanks.' Phil tossed some cod in batter. 'But now give it a rest, right?'

Vicki and Peter had strolled out to the *Storm Goddess*, hoping they might think of some way of sneaking on to the ship that night.

Vicki had finished reading the first mate's journal before they went out. She now saw the *Storm Goddess* with new eyes. It struck her, for example, that there was only one lifeboat secured amidships on the starboard side. She scrutinized the rope ladder on the port side. Twenty men had gone down it and back again, so it would almost certainly hold if she and Peter used it to climb aboard.

Sergeant Willis, who had removed his helmet and was sunning himself outside the door of the police camper van, was glaring at them malevolently. Of course. The police still suspected them of wanting to get on board the ship. Whoever was on duty tonight would keep his eyes peeled.

'Do you know who's on duty tonight?' Vicki asked Phil.

He shook his head. 'Not my uncle, anyway. Not Willis, either.'

'No?'

'I heard it this morning, when I was over at the police station with my uncle. The harbour master came in and gave them both the night off – said they couldn't be expected to stand guard around the clock. When my uncle asked who would be on duty, the harbour master said, "Not your problem, I've made arrangements."'

Vicki and Peter looked at each other. So now they would have an unknown guard to deal with. Or, if they were very unlucky, two of them.

'This time,' said Peter, 'we're going to need a whole heap of luck. All we can get.'

'Are you really planning to have another go?' Phil asked Vicki.

'I *have* to.' She ran her eyes over the *Storm Goddess*. 'And I want to.'

SIXTEEN

There wasn't a cloud in the sky when Vicki and Peter stealthily crept along the quay. The moon was as dazzlingly bright as a fog lamp, and the bay's broad expanse was so flooded with light that every little fold in the mud flats was visible.

Brilliantly illuminated by the floodlights as well as the moon, the *Storm Goddess* loomed in the middle of the bay, a bulky, commanding shape.

As Vicki stood looking over at the ship from the top of the quay, she suddenly realized that she herself was bathed in light. She was overcome by the sensation of being watched. Eyes seemed to be staring at her from all around the bay. She could actually feel them pricking her like needles.

'Let's go.' Taking Peter's hand, she urged him quickly down the slipway to the beach.

But it was just as light down there, and when they set off across the mud flats they would be crossing an entirely level expanse. They would be easily visible for miles, but they couldn't crawl up to the ship on their bellies. Vicki looked at Peter, who was proceeding at a crouch and peering around as if in search of potential pursuers. When he caught her looking at him, he straightened up and gave a wry smile. 'Now I know how a bug under a microscope must feel. Not a very nice sensation.'

She nodded.

In her case, the unpleasant sensations had started that afternoon. Peter had gone off at lunchtime to join his parents, and she'd tried to while away the time till he returned without thinking about tonight. But it was no use. Nothing took her mind off it, neither the computer game her grandmother had given her for Christmas, nor her favorite CDs. Even her *Hornblower* books had failed to do the trick. Serving in the restaurant would have been the thing, but Dad didn't need her, the new waitress was proving to be so quick and efficient.

When Peter finally showed up, which he did much later than expected, he wasn't in the best of moods either. Although he'd spent the afternoon with his parents and had dinner with them, they hadn't wanted him to sleep over again. They had allowed him to come only when he swore that this would be the very last time.

Now Peter and Vicki were walking together across the mud flats in this almost unnatural brightness, nagged by the uneasy feeling that they were being watched by a hundred pairs of eyes.

And they had no idea what they'd find when they reached the ship.

The guards, for a start. Would they manage to sneak past them? Who would they be? Some policemen from another station, or had the harbour master employed a security firm? In any case, they would probably have to reckon with more than one. Vicki strained her eyes. She could make out the police camper van, but no details yet. On the other hand, it was quite possible that the guards had already spotted her and Peter and were watching them through binoculars. They would have to crawl the final stretch – *if* they got that far.

The *Storm Goddess* loomed up ahead like a mute challenge.

Vicki couldn't remember ever having felt so uneasy while crossing the mud flats.

Phil was anxious.

It was after midnight, and he was sitting on a bench on

the quay overlooking the deserted square in front of the town hall, worrying about Vicki. About her friend Peter too, of course, but mainly about Vicki, whom he'd known ever since opening his first burger van, which served burgers of all kinds, hot dogs and French fries. She'd appeared one day, a tot too small to see over the counter, and asked for some battered cod. When he'd suggested some French fries instead, she'd turned up her nose and said, 'I thought we'd finally got somewhere that sold some decent fish and chips.' Vicki had alerted him to a gap in the market, so to speak. She was a frequent visitor to his trailer these days – and she could now see over the counter easily.

A little while earlier Phil had sat on the quay and watched the two figures making their way across the mud flats towards the *Storm Goddess*. They were a long way off, but he could easily make them out on this remarkably moonlit night.

He'd offered to accompany them that evening – not that he was all that keen after hearing his uncle tell the harbour master about the blood. But Vicki had said that three of them would never be able to stay hidden. She was right, and Phil had been almost relieved not to have to go too. But he'd resolved to hold himself in readiness. If Vicki and Peter got into trouble out there – if there was a repetition of that horrific fight – he would go to their rescue. As soon as they reached the ship he intended to follow them out there on his bicycle.

Until then he could relax on the bench. His bike was in a shadowy dip in the sand below the quay. The light was really odd tonight, he reflected. Almost as bright as daylight, but different. The shadows were darker – black as ink. The town hall entrance was nearly as visible as it would have been by day, but the circular bench beneath the big plane tree, although close to where Phil was sitting, could scarcely be seen.

How far would the two of them have managed to get by now? He rose and walked over to the railings. There they were, two tiny, solitary figures out on the mud flats. They were just over halfway there.

Phil went back to his bench.

Vicki and Peter had squatted down and were staring at the camper van beyond the chain-link fence. There was a light on inside, but Vicki couldn't see any guards.

'See anyone?' she asked, whispering nervously. Although they were still quite a distance from the ship, they could hear the generator humming away.

Peter shook his head. 'Not with the naked eye, at any rate.' He fished his miniature telescope out of his jeans.

Putting it to his eye, he carefully scanned the sand surrounding the *Storm Goddess*. 'No one outside. They must be in the van.'

'Fine, let's go!' They walked on, keeping low. As before, they made a detour to the right so that Phil's trailer would screen them from anybody watching. But they still had a way to go.

While walking, Vicki kept her eye on the camper van as best she could, ready to throw herself flat at a moment's notice, but there was no sign of movement.

They broke into a run. A few more metres, and they'd made it; they were out of sight. But only for the moment, because it wouldn't be long before someone came out to patrol the fence. They would be spotted for certain – unless they were under cover by then.

A final dash for Phil's trailer, and they'd made it

Panting hard, they crouched down outside the back door, the way they had the night before. They were safe for the moment. What next?

'I vote we wait till one of the guards has done his rounds,' Peter whispered. Vicki nodded.

They waited. For ages.

Nothing happened.

They waited some more.

'Great guards,' Vicki whispered. 'What are they doing,

sleeping? Shouldn't they be out on patrol?'

Peter stared up at the roof of the trailer. 'I could take a look inside,' he whispered.

'Inside what?'

'The camper van. I'm sure I could see inside from up there.' He got to his feet. 'Cup your hands.' Vicki did so. He caught hold of the roof bars and hauled himself up. She watched him open-mouthed. So he was athletic as well as brainy!

Peter lay flat on the roof, peering through his telescope. Vicki held her breath. What if a guard came out now? But Peter took his time.

Then he got up, turned around, and sat there with his legs dangling over the edge. He was sitting there in full view of the van!

'Peter! Are you crazy?'

'You won't believe it.' He pocketed his telescope, then pushed off and jumped to the ground. 'It's empty,' he announced. 'The camper van's empty. There isn't a soul inside.'

'No one?' Vicki drew a deep breath. So there weren't any guards at all! They could easily climb over the chain-link fence and . . . just a minute. The harbour master had given the police the night off and he hadn't sent any replacements. He'd made sure someone could get aboard the ship undisturbed, and he wouldn't have done that for their benefit.

Peter realized this at the same moment Vicki did. They darted to the corner of the trailer and looked back across the mud flats.

There he was.

Belper was striding towards them, fast.

Exactly twenty minutes earlier, Phil had glanced at his watch and decided that it was time to follow his friends out to the ship. And then, just as he got to his feet, the door of the town hall had opened. Quickly, he crouched down behind the bench and squinted through the slats.

It was the harbour master and the bald-headed man, Belper.

Belper was waving his arms about and saying something to the harbour master in low but insistent tones. The harbour master shook his head several times, which seemed to infuriate Belper, who suddenly raised his voice. 'You're simply making excuses. You know what? You're scared, that's all. Too scared to come with me.'

Come with him where? Phil listened intently.

The harbour master looked around, then drew Belper into the shade of the plane tree. 'Listen to me,' he said quietly but menacingly. 'For the last time: your job is to find the gold, mine is to cover your back. Got it?'

So Belper was planning to get on board the ship, tonight of all nights, when Vicki and Peter were out there.

Luckily, thought Phil, I'll be able to warn them in good time.

'Call me when you've found the stuff,' the harbour master went on, 'and I'll come and help you remove it.'

Of course. He knew what Belper might come up against on board. The harbour master was a crafty piece of work; he was using the man as cannon fodder.

'Thanks a bunch!' Belper was getting steadily angrier. 'And for that you expect a half share? Outrageous!' he hissed. 'Don't forget the gold is my property!'

'*Your* property? Don't make me laugh. It belongs to the government.'

'That's a gross injustice! I won't stand for it. No one's going to rob my family of that gold a second time, I promise you. You should be ashamed of yourself, disputing my right to it. *Your* ancestor robbed *mine*. He was nothing but a pirate.'

'And what was yours? A slave trader, thank you very much!'

'The slave trade was legal in the eighteenth century.'

'So? It was a dirty business all the same. Look, let's cut the chatter. I've given you the keys, Belper, so get going.

And don't forget, this is your first and last chance to get aboard that wreck.'

'I'll find the goods,' Belper snarled. 'You can bet your life on that.'

The harbour master turned to go, then paused. 'Get this straight, Belper. If anything goes wrong, if you run into any problems, you're on your own. I'll say I strictly forbade you to search the ship, understand?'

'That's just what I expected of you.' Belper's voice took on a low, menacing note. 'You seriously think I haven't taken out some insurance?'

'Meaning what?'

'Meaning, my friend, that *you're* the one who should watch his step.' Belper abruptly turned on his heel, stalked off, and disappeared down the quayside. The harbour master stood looking after him for quite a while. Then he turned and strode back to the town hall, and he too disappeared.

Phil waited a few moments before running to the railings. Cautiously, he peered down over the mud flats.

Belper was standing on the beach below, gazing out across the bay at the *Storm Goddess*. Just as Phil spotted him, he set off at a brisk pace.

Phil got out his mobile and dialled. 'Hi, you've reached Vicki,' he heard. 'Please leave me a message. Thanks.' Vicki had turned her phone off. Of course. What now?

Should he ride after Baldilocks? 'Hey, Mr Belper, I know what you're up to, so turn back – and make it snappy, if you don't mind, or I'll be forced to give you a sock on the jaw.' It didn't take a lot of imagination to figure out what the result of that would be.

What, then? Should he simply overtake Belper on his bike and warn the pair of them? The trouble was, Vicki had said she *had* to get aboard. He couldn't afford to mess things up for her.

No, he had no choice. Phil gazed across the mud flats at the *Storm Goddess*. He would wait a while, then ride in pursuit so as to be on the spot if needed – as long as he got there in time.

SEVENTEEN

Vicki and Peter had crouched down and were peering round the end of Phil's trailer. Belper was still striding across the mud flats toward the *Storm Goddess*.

Vicki suddenly felt depressed and disheartened. They'd been lucky enough to find the police trailer deserted, but now this guy had reappeared to ruin everything. A man as rapacious as Belper would stop at nothing.

She shook her head. They weren't going to give up yet. The camper van was only deserted because Belper wanted to get aboard the ship. No point in crying over spilled milk. It was better to work out what to do next.

'Well?' said Peter. 'We'll have to have a rethink.' He paused. 'To be honest, I'm not too keen on meeting up with that man.'

That meant running away. They would never get another chance to board the *Storm Goddess*, that was for sure. Vicki stared across the mud flats.

Belper still had around half the distance to cover, so it would be a while before he got there. Not long, though, at the speed he was walking. Vicki had to decide fast. 'Let's climb on board,' she said, looking at Peter. 'All right?'

Peter hesitated for a moment. 'All right. We'll go on board.' He uttered the words slowly and firmly, as if making a solemn vow.

They sprinted over to the fence and scaled it as quickly as they had the first time.

Now for the ladder.

Vicki took hold of the ropes on either side, put her foot on the lowest rung – and hesitated. Was there any reason why she shouldn't climb on to the ship? Had she overlooked something?

'Anything wrong?' Peter whispered from behind her.

She was about to shake her head when . . . wait, could she hear voices? She strained her ears. No, just the hum of the generator. 'Everything's fine,' she said, and started climbing.

Just below the bulwarks, she stopped short. She wasn't going to jump down on deck as hurriedly as the last time. Slowly raising her head, she peeked over the edge. All clear. No one in sight, nothing lying around, everything securely lashed down, and the planks were spotless – they looked as if they'd been freshly scrubbed. The pool of blood beside the forward companionway seemed to have vanished without a trace, and there wasn't a stain to be seen beside the mainmast, where the first mate had been sitting in Vicki's dream.

Over on the starboard side, a flight of steps led up to the afterdeck. There was nothing stowed beneath the steps, which Vicki found surprising. She'd taken it for granted that every nook and cranny aboard an ocean-going sailing ship would be occupied. Beside the steps was a door that gave access to the compartments beneath the afterdeck and to the captain's cabin. Nearer the middle was the aft companionway. The hatch cover was battened down as if in expectation of heavy seas.

'What is it?' Peter whispered. He was halfway up the rope ladder just below her.

'Nothing,' Vicki whispered back. 'Just looking around first.'

The deck looked deserted and innocuous, but what would happen when she actually set foot on it? The first mate and the rest of the crew were waiting for her to lift the curse, so she'd be welcome, wouldn't she?

But what if the captain's men and the first mate's men

were fighting? She and Peter would find themselves in the middle of a blood bath. She couldn't count on nothing happening to them.

Vicki was gripped by fear once more.

She looked down at Peter, who was staring up at her tensely. She could hardly tell him, 'Peter, I've changed my mind, let me down.' What kind of fool would she look, and not just to him but to herself?

Besides, the first mate was waiting. She was sure of it.

She looked up, then quickly climbed the last few rungs and lowered herself from the bulwark to the deck.

Almost instantly she was overcome by a feeling that invisible tentacles were clutching at her, clinging to her like limpets, gripping her on all sides, slithering up the companionways, coming up through the deck. They seemed to enfold her in a tight embrace that would never be released. She gasped and opened her mouth to scream, but that was when she heard the voices.

The tentacles relaxed their grip.

The voices were coming from behind a door. The captain and the first mate were arguing in the stern cabin.

She still couldn't catch what they were saying, but it wouldn't be long before they raised their voices. And then . . . Vicki looked around. Where could they hide? There was only one possible place. She heard Peter land on the deck behind her. 'Quick!' she whispered. 'Under the steps over there!'

They darted across the deck and scrambled beneath the steps leading to the afterdeck. Although they were in shadow there, it wasn't much of a hiding place. Anyone who happened to look in their direction would be bound to spot them, and they were close to the door that led aft. Frighteningly close.

The voices in the captain's cabin had risen. 'Where are they, those doubloons?!' roared the captain. 'You had no right to take them, you and your cronies. Where have you hidden them?'

'I won't tell you!' said the first mate. He spoke quietly, but it sounded as if he was forcing himself to remain calm. 'That gold isn't rightfully ours. It'll be the ruin of us!'

'For the last time,' the captain bellowed, 'where are those doubloons?!'

'You can search the ship from stem to stern,' said the first mate, louder now. 'You'll never find them!' A chair scraped on the deck.

Beneath the steps, Vicki and Peter cowered back as far as they could go. Peter was staring at the door, wide-eyed.

'Come back here!' the captain shouted angrily. A door slammed. 'Come back, you dog!'

The door beside their hiding place was flung open

so violently that it rebounded off the steps and slammed shut.

There stood the first mate. Pigtail, loose-sleeved white shirt, sea boots with their tops turned down. He was standing with his back to them, but Vicki could see that he was breathing heavily. He had a cutlass in his hand, and he was gripping the hilt so tightly that his knuckles looked whitish in the gloom.

Without looking around, he ran to the forward companionway, where he came to a halt. The hatch cover over this companionway was also closed. He turned round and looked back at the door. But for one brief moment, Vicki felt quite certain, his eyes had rested on *her*. The first mate knew she was on board.

The door burst open and slammed shut again. The captain had emerged.

He really was a giant of a man. Tall three-cornered hat, knee-length blue coat gathered at the waist, buckled shoes. He wore his cutlass on a belt beneath his coat, and he was holding a pistol. It looked just like a pistol from a pirate film.

He was standing so near the door that Vicki could see his face. It wasn't smooth, but pitted as if the sea had eaten it away, like the face of the portrait in the Seashell. Unlike that face, however, it was contorted with rage.

The captain raised his pistol, aimed it at the first mate, and pulled the trigger.

At such close range the report was ear-splitting, and the muzzle of the pistol belched a fireball of orange flame.

Missed!

The first mate still stood there, cutlass in hand.

The captain brandished his pistol in the air. 'Come on, men, to arms!' he yelled. 'Show these cowardly mutineers! Save your gold!'

The first mate raised his cutlass. 'On deck, all who fear God and the law! Show these lawbreakers! Save the ship!'

At that, the hatch cover over the forward companionway flew open and out sprang a seaman in a flat, round hat, he too with a cutlass in his hand. Behind him came a man in a leather apron swinging an axe, and another man, and another.

More men emerged from the aft companionway and joined the captain, also armed with pistols and cutlasses. All that could still be heard was the sound of their feet pounding the deck, but in a moment the shouting would start, and then . . .

'Inside, quick!' Vicki hissed.

They darted in through the nearby door and cowered back against the wooden bulkhead. At that moment, shouts rent the air outside. A babble of voices arose, mingled with the clash of steel against steel and the muffled thud of blows being exchanged.

They obviously hadn't been seen. No one followed them. They were in a cabin bathed in the glow from the moon and the floodlights outside, which was streaming in through a big corner window, and in spite of the frightful din outside, Vicki managed to absorb her surroundings. A large table, flanked by benches, suggested that this was the mess where the ship's officers took their meals and assembled for meetings, and the door at the far end, which displayed some painted decoration, probably led to the captain's cabin. Beside it was another door, a plain plank door pierced by two ventilation slits the width of a man's hand. A storeroom? Hanging from a hook beside it was a rectangular lantern made of iron, and burning inside its little windows was a fat candle. Of course, this must be the . . .

Bang!

The gunshot transfixed Vicki like a thunderbolt. It was the second gunshot, so she should have been prepared for it – and for the terrible cries that followed, which seemed once more to go on for ever. Unable to restrain herself, she stole to the doorway and looked out.

It was the man in the flat hat. He was rolling around beside the forward companionway, screaming incessantly.

Vicki darted back.

She pressed up against the bulkhead, listening to the screams and thinking that this shouldn't be happening, that it wasn't real, that it was only going on in her head. But it wasn't, because Peter was standing beside her, hearing what she was hearing. He was leaning against the bulkhead, silent and wide-eyed. At that moment, the screams died away.

Peter stared at the deck, white as a sheet. He looked up. 'Vicki,' he whispered, 'what do you think? Could *we* get hit by a shot like that?'

A shot like that . . . ? Vicki immediately became aware of the danger they were in. Even if they remained unnoticed by the two sides, they weren't immune to stray bullets.

'We need to find a hiding place,' she whispered back. 'A good one.' She paused. 'A *really* good one.'

Phil felt relieved.

Looking across the mud flats as he sat on the quay, he could see that Belper still had a fair way to go. He would set off on his bike so as to reach the *Storm Goddess* in good time – just in case Vicki and Peter got into a jam. Not that he thought it likely.

They must have climbed on board the ship long ago, and he hadn't heard a thing. No horrific pools of blood this time, or so it seemed. That was why he was feeling pretty relaxed.

All that still worried him was why Vicki wanted to get on to the wreck in the first place. Why was she putting herself in danger? Even she didn't know the answer; she'd said so more than once. 'I *have* to,' she'd said, 'and I want to.' Besides, she seemed to know exactly what she was doing. Phil wished she'd taken him into her confidence. Then he would have a better idea of how to help her. Still, the fewer people who knew the *Storm Goddess*'s secret the better, he realized that.

He, Phil, knew it. He wasn't stupid. He'd overheard Vicki telling Peter about the photograph inside the head at the table behind his fish and chip stand. The rest he'd worked out for himself. Vicki was in a pretty tricky situation – one from which she and Peter would find it hard to extricate themselves on their own. If they succeeded, it would matter quite a lot to the people who lived around the bay, or so Phil believed. And it would also matter to himself. That was another reason why he was helping Vicki – not just because he liked her. Well, he thought, looking at his thickly bandaged thumb, he'd done his bit so far.

Then he heard the shouts.

They weren't very loud, but they were clearly audible. They obviously came from the ship, but was this really a repetition of last night's performance? He listened hard. Moments later, a shot rang out.

Phil jumped up and ran down the slipway to the dip in the sand where he'd left his bike. As he was picking it up his eye strayed to the top of the quay. The harbour master had reappeared and was standing there. Instantly, Phil threw himself flat on the sand, bicycle and all. Had the harbour master seen him? Cautiously, he peered over the edge of the dip.

Phil watched the harbour master stare out at the *Storm Goddess*, then tear his eyes away and scan the road along the top of the quay in both directions. There was no one in sight. He turned and checked the square in front of the town hall. No one there, either. He looked back at the ship again. After a while, he turned away and disappeared behind the town hall.

As quickly as he could, Phil pushed his bike across the sand until he reached firmer ground. Then he rode off.

Vicki and Peter were feeling relatively safe. Their hiding place wasn't the *really* good one Vicki had hoped for, but it was adequate. Anyway, beggars couldn't be choosers.

They both knew that they shouldn't venture outside while the fighting was going on. On the other hand, the wooden bulkhead that separated them from the deck amidships was too thin to stop a bullet. The storeroom and cupboard behind the plank door were also out of the question, because they lay behind the same bulkhead. That left the captain's cabin.

Vicki darted over to the door painted with images of the sea and opened it a crack. The captain's cabin had a big stern window with a couple of sea chests standing beneath it. Over to one side, flanked by several chairs, stood a table with a metal pitcher and two mugs on it. On the opposite wall Vicki saw a big, unmade bunk with a pillow and quilt of some blue checked material. The captain *lived* here, it occurred to her. These were his private quarters. No, they couldn't hide in here – he might return at any moment! She quickly shut the door and shook her head at Peter.

He was standing beside the plain wooden door. It was stouter than it looked and had a lock, but there was no key. Peter lifted the latch, and the door swung open. He poked his head inside and gave a startled exclamation. Vicki followed him.

Running along the outer wall of the windowless compartment was a wooden rack, and in it, resting on their butts in a row, were muskets. There must have been at least two dozen of them – heavy, long-barrelled weapons like the ones in the local museum. But this was no museum.

Peter stared at the muskets. 'They're the real thing!' he

said. 'Someone's bound to come in and fetch them any minute!' He turned. 'We'd better get out of here! Back on deck, quick!'

But Vicki held him by the sleeve. She had also been startled at first, but then it struck her that she'd never seen a pirate film in which muskets were used. Cutlasses and pistols, yes; muskets, no. 'No,' she said quickly. They'd already spent far too long looking for a hiding place. 'Those things are too big and unwieldy. They won't use them for fighting at close range.'

Although Peter didn't seem too convinced, he crouched down behind the rack with her. They had no choice. At least they felt reasonably safe behind the close-packed row of guns, which formed a kind of barrier. They had shut the door to the officers' mess, but the ventilation slits let in a fair amount of light.

Beside the door was another hook for a lantern. The walls were lined with shelves bearing wooden boxes and items of equipment whose function Vicki didn't know. On one of the shelves against the outer wall was a row of containers, seemingly of wood but resembling bottles squashed flat. Powder flasks! They were filled with gunpowder.

Silence had fallen outside on deck. But the silence wasn't absolute. Vicki and Peter could hear footsteps, hatches being opened and closed. If Vicki held her breath she could hear men panting from their exertions. The deck below them was also being searched.

'What if they look in here?' Peter whispered.

Vicki listened to the noises around them, noises she'd heard before. Of course! 'Even if they find us,' she whispered back, 'I don't think they'll hurt us.'

'What makes you think that?'

'They're doomed to do exactly what they did during their last fight, so they *can't* do anything to us.'

'But what if this fight *isn't* their last fight? What if it's another fight – not the one they fought two centuries ago?'

'Why should it be?'

'Because *you're* on board.'

He had a point. But in that case, what then? Vicki thought hard. Then it came to her. 'Even if they are capable of harming us, why should they? They want me to lift the curse on them.'

But Peter shook his head. 'Not necessarily. Maybe the captain doesn't *want* it lifted – maybe that's *part* of the curse.'

True, thought Vicki, that was another possibility. But what could they do? Vicki couldn't think of anything useful. All they could do was wait, huddled together, and hope that no one would come in.

Abruptly, the din outside resumed. Once more they heard a confused hubbub, the clash of steel on steel and the muffled thud of blows being exchanged. And, as before, the yells of the combatants sounded so horrific, so savage and ferocious, that Vicki put her fingers in her ears and prayed for the noise to stop.

What next? She couldn't just hide in this oversized cupboard and wait for ever. She had come aboard to release the crew of the *Storm Goddess* from their curse. You didn't lift a curse simply by sitting around. She had to do something, but what?

The trouble was, for the moment they were stuck. She couldn't risk venturing out into the thick of the fighting, so she continued to crouch behind the musket rack, listening to the racket outside and wondering what her next move should be.

And then the din died down again. It seemed as if the men were searching for any of their enemies who might have taken cover.

How would the whole thing end?

All Vicki knew was that she and the first mate were destined to meet again. But what could *she* do to help? What was expected of her?

And then she heard footsteps.

They were very close. Someone had entered the officers'

mess. Involuntarily, Vicki and Peter cowered still lower –
not that it would do them much good, because they only
had the narrow side of the musket rack to hide behind.

The footsteps came closer. They were just outside the
door.

The door opened.

The first thing Vicki saw was the lantern that had been
hanging on the hook outside. Someone was using it to
illuminate the arms store.

Then, bending low because of his height, a man came in.

Vicki stifled a scream.

It was the captain.

EIGHTEEN

Vicki crouched behind the musket rack, clearly exposed to the captain's gaze, staring up at him. Straightening up, the captain hung the lantern on the inner hook and turned to face the shelf lined with the boxes and powder flasks. He took a step towards it, then came to a halt.

By the look of him, he seemed to be pondering something that had just occurred to him.

But his eyes were fixed on Vicki.

He was staring straight at her.

She realized that, for the first time in her life, she was gazing into the eyes of a truly evil person.

Looking at his pitted, weather-beaten face, she saw that the veins in his forehead and neck were swelling – and suddenly she understood.

The captain was wrestling with himself.

He was fighting the curse he lay under, trying to escape from the preordained series of movements and actions to which he had been doomed. He was striving to do what he wanted to do.

Which was kill her.

Vicki crouched there, stiff and motionless.

The captain's face flushed still more, and his eyes rolled. Then he suddenly uttered a groan. His body jerked violently and he began to move.

Going over to the shelf, he picked up a box and one of the powder flasks, went back to the door, took the lantern from the hook, and went out.

Vicki slumped against the bulkhead.

Beside her, Peter expelled a deep breath. 'That was awful,' he whispered. 'But at least we now know they can't harm us.'

Vicki nodded feebly, but she was far from convinced. Would the captain have fought against the curse so hard if he hadn't thought he could break it? He could obviously control his eyes. Why not the rest of his body?

Peter tiptoed to the door and peered through one of the ventilation slits. He beckoned Vicki over.

The captain had placed the lantern at one end of the mess table and was busy with his pistol at the other. Having poured some powder from the wooden flask into the muzzle, he took a bullet from the box and inserted it in the barrel followed by a wad, them tamped the charge down with a ramrod.

All Vicki saw at first was that the captain was reloading his pistol – he'd fired it right at the outset and missed, of course. But then it occurred to her that she knew who the bullet was meant for. And there was no changing it – or so she would have thought before the captain had looked at her. At that point, she'd still believed she must witness the fight aboard the *Storm Goddess* without being able to affect its outcome in the slightest. She wasn't so sure any more. But what *could* she do? What was *expected* of her?

The captain checked the flint in the hammer of his pistol, then put the weapon in an inside pocket and quit the officers' mess. He left the lantern burning on the table, as if he would need it later.

Vicki listened. Silence had fallen outside. Was the fight nearly over, or would the uproar break out again?

As before, the silence wasn't absolute. She thought she could hear footsteps up above, and others were audible on the deck below.

There . . . someone was opening a hatch. The one over the aft companionway. She heard someone descending the stairs, then footsteps on the deck beneath her. That must be where the officers' cabins were. A door creaked open.

Should they wait any longer? There might still be some survivors. What if one of them succeeded in breaking the curse? Or more than one? Perhaps the captain would too.

But if the fight really was coming to an end she must go outside. There was no alternative: she and the first mate had to meet once more.

Vicki strained her ears again. All that broke the silence were some creaking sounds. It was impossible to tell where they were coming from. Were the ship's timbers simply creaking as she settled in the mud?

Enough of this. She had to make a move sometime. 'Peter,' she whispered, 'I was called on to the ship because I'm supposed to do something – I don't know what, but I certainly can't do anything in here. I have to go outside.'

'OK,' Peter whispered back. 'The crew may start fighting again, but we'll have to risk it. At least they can't harm us.'

Vicki merely nodded. She didn't have the nerve to tell him, not now, that she took a rather different view of the matter.

Peter opened the door, looked around briefly, and then darted over to another door leading to the deck. Vicki followed him.

Cautiously, he put his head out, and quickly shrank back.

'I, ah . . . ' he said, turning pale. He leaned against the bulkhead for support.

'What is it?' Vicki whispered. He gestured mutely at the doorway. She looked through it, too – and recoiled just as he had.

The deck was littered with bodies. Dead bodies.

Vicki drew several deep breaths. Although she'd known that this was a fight that none of the *Storm Goddess*'s crew had survived, it hadn't occurred to her that their corpses would really and truly be strewn around all over the place. She squared her shoulders. 'Shall we go outside?'

Peter nodded. 'Sure. I was just surprised, that's all.'

They went out on deck. Vicki pointed to the steps they'd hidden under, and Peter nodded again. She shut the door to the officers' mess so it wouldn't block their view. But she kept her eyes fixed on the deck as they made their way to the steps, and once there she avoided looking directly at any of the bodies. The door to the aft companionway was open, Vicki saw, whereas that of the forward companionway was shut. Sprawled on the deck beside it was the man who had screamed so horribly. She couldn't help seeing the big pool of blood in which he lay.

If she was unlucky, some survivors might set on each other before her eyes. She hoped she would be spared that sight.

But there was *one* fight she would *have* to watch. The fight that would take place last of all.

Phil was feeling more and more apprehensive.

Lying flat on his stomach on the roof of his trailer, eyes fixed on the window of the police camper van, he was watching Belper's preparations with mounting anxiety.

The man was getting some tools together. He put an axe and a handsaw on the table, followed by a hammer, a jemmy and a crowbar – he obviously thought the gold must be hidden beneath some of the decking. The tools were part of the camper van's emergency equipment, and the rucksack in which he stowed them had probably been dumped there in advance. He ignored the aluminium ladder lying on the floor of the van. Of course, Phil remembered, there was a rope ladder with wooden rungs hanging down the ship's side. Belper shouldered the backpack, took a big torch from a shelf, and made his way outside, locking the door behind him.

Phil flattened himself against the roof although he knew that, at this moment, Belper was oblivious to what was happening around him on the mud flats. Phil had easily managed to slip past the man, bike and all. Belper hadn't spared his surroundings a glance, just circled the ship several times, then halted beside the rope ladder and looked up. He seemed focused on a single idea: getting aboard and finding the hidden gold.

At the same time, however, he appeared surprisingly cautious. He'd waited until the bloodcurdling noises from the ship had died away. Belper wasn't stupid – he had no desire to become embroiled in any hand-to-hand fighting. He didn't believe in the story of a distant pirate film, that was for sure. The townspeople obviously did, because none of them, not even that woman reporter, had bothered to come and take a look around. The policemen hadn't, either, but they were off duty. As for the harbour master, he wouldn't show up until the gold was found.

The noises from the ship gradually faded. Belper prepared to climb the ladder, then stopped short. Sounds were still coming from on board. Footsteps could be heard, hatch covers were being opened and closed. Belper remained standing at the foot of the rope ladder and waited a while longer.

Phil intended to follow Belper as soon as he climbed on to the ship, so as to be on hand when he came across Vicki and Peter. Belper wouldn't want any witnesses around while he was looking for his gold, and Phil thought it unlikely that the youngsters would get away unharmed. That was what worried him most of all. Phil kept his eyes on Belper at the foot of the ladder.

Phil's main concern at first had been that something might happen to Vicki and Peter. If Belper hadn't been watching the ship like a hawk, Phil would have climbed up at once and gone to check on the pair. But the longer the racket went on, the more clearly he'd realized that he couldn't simply intervene, especially as he had a strong suspicion that Vicki wouldn't want him to. He'd heard nothing from them since reaching the scene, no screams or cries for help; he took that as a good sign.

On the other hand, having watched Belper for a while, he realized that the man would stop at nothing to get his hands on the gold.

The sounds on board had now ceased altogether. All was quiet up there.

Belper clipped the torch to his belt, and started to climb the ladder.

Phil got ready to jump down. As soon as Belper was out of sight he would sprint over to the ladder and shinny up it in double-quick time.

Belper was halfway up when he froze.

Footsteps could be heard coming from the ship.

The footsteps were echoing from below deck.

Vicki looked at the aft companionway. Who would it be? Whoever it was, she could hear him climbing the steps.

And then . . . no, no three-cornered hat.

It was the first mate.

He emerged from the companionway and came out on deck. He had stuck his cutlass in his belt and was holding something under his left arm: a black packet tied up with string. Vicki stared at it. Could it be *the* packet?

She tried to catch the first mate's eye, but he wasn't looking at her; more precisely, he hadn't turned his head in her direction. She understood why: he hadn't done so two centuries ago, so he couldn't do so now.

Taking the packet in both hands, he walked across the deck. Carefully stepping over the dead bodies, he carried the packet toward the port bulwark, where the rope ladder was hanging. He was three paces from it when a crash split the air. He swung round.

The hatch cover over the forward companionway had been thrown open.

The captain's hat appeared. His face was twisted with fury. 'Cornered you at last, you traitor!' he cried.

'Well, what of your gold?' the first mate retorted. 'Have you found it?' He was standing quite still with the packet in both hands, watching the captain.

'I'll find it yet. But first I shall dispatch you on your final voyage. I see you've already packed your bundle for the journey, you mutinous dog, so go to the devil!'

Everything happened very quickly after that.

The captain reached beneath his coat and whipped out his cutlass, and the first mate dropped the packet and drew his own cutlass before the packet hit the deck.

Later, much later, Vicki would wonder why she hadn't shut her eyes. At that moment, however, the possibility never entered her head. She watched, spellbound, as the captain rushed wildly at the first mate with his cutlass levelled; saw the first mate sidestep his oncoming opponent, almost playfully deflect the blade with his own, and send him charging past into thin air.

The captain's momentum took him almost as far as the ship's side. He swung back, quick as lightning, but the first mate was on him in a flash and ran him through.

The captain went rigid, his bulging eyes fixed on the first mate's face. He continued to grip his weapon as if about to launch another attack, then gave a bubbling cry and toppled over on his back.

The first mate's cutlass was buried in his chest.

'Go to the devil yourself,' said the first mate.

Without a backward glance, he turned and retraced his steps to where the packet was lying.

As she watched him go, Vicki caught a sudden movement out of the corner of her eye and turned to look. The captain was stirring! Dumbfounded at first, then horrified, she saw him sit up with the cutlass still embedded in his chest. He reached inside his coat and produced the pistol.

The first mate was just bending down to retrieve the packet.

Vicki let out a cry.

She heard herself. She didn't know what she shouted, but she shouted it at the top of her lungs.

The first mate spun round, clasping the packet to his chest with both hands. He was facing the spot where the captain was sitting, but the first mate wasn't looking at him.

He was looking at Vicki.

'Who called me?' he asked. He asked the question quite calmly and without surprise, as if he already knew the answer. The answer he'd been seeking for so long.

Then a shot rang out.

The impact of the bullet knocked the first mate backwards and sent him crashing to the deck. He uttered a long sigh.

Silence followed.

The man lay on his back without moving. He was still holding the packet in both hands.

The captain, too, was now lying still with the cutlass protruding from his chest and the discharged pistol beside him.

Vicki looked again at the first mate. He hadn't stirred. What was the matter with him? He *couldn't* be dead. The fight *couldn't* end this way. Please don't be dead, she thought. I haven't been able to do a thing. Please . . . and then the first mate moved.

Slowly, he rolled over on his side and began to groan the way he'd groaned in the attic. The front of his shirt was dark with blood. He struggled to sit up. Vicki could see that he was summoning up all his strength in an effort to rise.

Should she help him? Was that it?

But the sailor rose unaided and stood there, swaying, but back on his feet. With the packet clasped to his chest, he tottered over to the bulwark from which the rope ladder was suspended, where he paused and braced himself.

Then he threw the packet overboard.

Phil was struggling to keep his nerve.

To put it bluntly, he was fighting back panic.

Vicki had screamed!

He had to save her. He had to go and help her right away. She was probably lying there on deck, hurt and bleeding. Peter was only a boy – he couldn't help her. She needed him, Phil, and if she *was* bleeding, every second counted.

But he couldn't help her.

He couldn't get to her because Belper was in the way. He was condemned to look on helplessly from the shelter of his trailer because the wretched man had frozen halfway up the rope ladder and wasn't budging an inch.

Phil had seen Belper move only twice since he'd stopped climbing: once when he'd looked up on hearing someone aboard the ship say, 'Well, what of your gold? Have you found it?' and a second time when something was tossed over the side. He'd started to climb down after it, but had obviously decided that it couldn't contain anything of interest to him after all. Belper had listened, motionless, to everything else that happened, including the fight between the two men, and the shot.

And Vicki's scream. Phil hadn't seen him show the slightest sign of emotion.

If only Belper hadn't locked the camper van. He'd left the gate in the fence open; Phil could have tried to sneak up the opposite side of the ship using the aluminium ladder.

Phil had naturally considered hurrying to the foot of the rope ladder and shouting, 'Let me up! That girl needs help!' But since Belper hadn't done what any decent person would have done – climb up and go to her aid – he certainly wouldn't let Phil go to the rescue.

And Vicki was still up there. She might even be injured.

Phil straightened up. He would have to use force. If

Belper didn't get down voluntarily, he would climb up after the man and yank him off the ladder by the ankles. But things could get tough on board the ship. He needed some means of self-defence, however makeshift. Something from the trailer? No, every second counted. Of course! Hurrying over to his bike, he released the seat shaft and pulled it out, complete with the seat, then weighed this improvised club in his hand. Not bad. Sticking it in his belt, he set off. He would have to be so quick that Belper wouldn't stand a chance.

Vicki!

That was her voice again.

Vicki was definitely up there on the deck.

'Does it hurt a lot?' Phil heard her ask.

NINETEEN

The first mate had swayed so violently when throwing the packet overboard that Vicki was afraid he would fall headlong. But he regained his balance, walked slowly over to the mainmast, and sat down. From the way he was groaning, he must be in terrible pain.

He was sitting facing the port side, so he couldn't see Vicki or Peter, who were huddled under the steps on the starboard side. To do so he would have had to turn his head, and that, thought Vicki, he hadn't done the first time she saw him. What would happen next? Had the time come for her to do something? Should she go over to him? If only he would give her some sign.

The first mate turned his head and looked at her — looked her straight in the eye. Then he turned away again.

272

Vicki got up.

She went over to him. Peter followed, which made her feel braver.

Vicki came to a halt in front of the first mate. He looked into her face. He didn't say anything, just sat there in silence with his back propped against the mast and his sea boots planted far apart. The front of his white, loose-sleeved shirt was dark with blood and blown apart, like the chest beneath . . . he continued to gaze at her.

Now she knew what she had to do.

It was the simplest thing in the world.

Slowly, she went right up to the first mate and laid a hand on his shoulder.

He closed his eyes, rested his head against the mast, and gave a deep sigh.

'Does it hurt a lot?' Vicki asked simply.

He opened his eyes, and it really seemed that he was smiling faintly. 'No,' he said, 'it doesn't hurt. Not any more.'

'That's good,' Vicki said, and sighed. Looking into the sailor's youthful face, she felt it fall away, all that had distressed and tormented her since coming aboard the *Storm Goddess*.

'Yes, it's good,' said the first mate, 'and you have played your part most admirably.' He looked at Peter, who was standing behind Vicki and a little to one side. 'You, too, have played your part exceeding well.'

'Thanks,' Peter said politely, coming to stand beside Vicki. Somehow he found it quite natural to express his thanks to an eighteenth-century sailor sitting mortally wounded with his back against the mast of a ghost ship. 'May I—' He broke off. 'May I ask you something?'

'You may, but I must tell you that my time here is short.'

'What will happen afterwards?' Vicki asked. 'I mean, when you've . . .'

'When I'm gone, you mean?' The first mate's gaze roamed across the corpses on deck and over to the bulwark, where the captain lay dead. 'I know not. I have my suspicions, but I know not.' He was looking at Vicki now. 'Whatever happens, I urge you both to quit this vessel immediately thereafter.' He turned to Peter. 'But you, too, had a question for me.'

'When the crew of the *Storm Goddess* fought their last fight again and again, did they know it?'

'Yes, we were doomed to do so. We fought the same fight countless times, and we always knew it. We were imprisoned in our own bodies – that was our punishment. Hell itself cannot be worse. At first it was my hope that we would sometime lose our minds, but even that mercy was denied us.' The first mate looked up at the sails. 'And we

274

soon abandoned hope that the ship would go down. She defied every storm but the last, which rent some of our canvas and carried us into this bay.' He looked at Vicki. 'That tempest, the sea's withdrawal, and my appearance in your garret – how, and by what power, those things were brought about is a secret to which I am not privy. Other things I do have knowledge of, so ask. But remember: my time here is short.'

Vicki would have been interested to learn if he knew about the picture of the hanged man inside the *Storm Goddess*'s head, but she would have to go into long-winded explanations if he didn't. In any case, the picture certainly wouldn't interest him at this point, when his sufferings would soon be over. What else would she like to know? 'That tear in the packet,' she said. 'What made it?'

'It was made by the pistol ball. The packet lessened its force, so it lodged inside me and stemmed the flow of blood a trifle.'

And she, Vicki, had been responsible for that. He wouldn't have turned around if she hadn't cried out. Was that good or bad?

The first mate had evidently read her thoughts. 'Can you not imagine?' He was really smiling now. 'You did the very thing you were meant to do. Had I not turned in response to your cry, the ball would have passed right through me, and I should not have been able to throw the packet over-board.'

Then it wouldn't have been washed ashore and the crew of the *Storm Goddess* would have been doomed for ever. But there was something wrong here. She'd called out only a moment ago.

'Yes, but I heard that cry of yours again and again. The first time it came to me from the future, but it is only now that I know who uttered it.'

So she'd called to him innumerable times . . . no, she herself hadn't, it was . . . Vicki shook her head. She mustn't think about it or she'd go dizzy again. She glanced at Peter standing beside her. He was gazing spellbound at the sailor, but *he* didn't look dizzy in the least. 'What about the gold?' he asked. 'Where had the captain hidden it? In his cabin?'

'No,' said the first mate. 'He would not have had to send the whole crew ashore for an entire day in order to hide it *there*. We were anchored off Santo Domingo on the island of Hispaniola. In those days the Caribbean was the chief market for the trade in slaves from Africa.'

'The Caribbean?' Peter shook his head. 'I didn't know that.'

'When the trader and his men came to fetch the slaves, the captain ordered us to row ashore, every man jack of us, and not to return until nightfall. At the time, I believed that he wished to conceal from us what price he had gotten for the slaves. Later, I realized he needed sufficient time to hide the gold.'

'So where *did* he hide it?' asked Vicki.

'The captain was taking precautions, after his own fashion. He wished to ensure that should anything happen to him on the homeward voyage – an ever-present possibility at sea – the gold would never be found. If *he* could not have it, nobody else could. So he chose a hiding place that no one would ever think of, or so he imagined.'

Vicki and Peter stared at the first mate expectantly.

'At the same time, this hiding place was in the nature of a cruel jest on the captain's part. It was a special place, one that all could see without ever suspecting what it concealed. The captain hid the gold, not within the ship, but without. It was—'

'Inside the figurehead!' cried Vicki.

'Within the *body* of the figurehead.'

'You don't say!' Peter looked awestruck. 'But how did you find out?'

'I bethought me that the captain had procured the new figurehead in three days. No one could have carved an entire figure in that time, only the head at most. The captain knew that too, of course. When the slave trader had departed with his cargo off Santo Domingo, he removed the head of the figure, together with the dowel that retained it, and enlarged the resulting cavity. It entailed a great deal of work, but it was practicable. Fifteen hundred doubloons are a vast fortune, but they take up little space.'

'And because the captain had removed the head,' said Vicki, 'it later came loose and had to be lashed to the aftermast.'

The first mate nodded. 'The plug remained in the body, so no one suspected anything even then.'

'No one except you,' said Peter. Then he asked the inevitable question – the one the first mate simply had to answer: 'So where did *you* hide the gold?'

'I did not hide it.'

No? Could he have deposited it somewhere in the open, the way Vicki had hidden his journal among her school books? But where on an ocean-going sailing ship could a fortune in gold be . . ?

Vicki and Peter grasped the truth at the same moment. They stared at the first mate, who nodded.

'The gold was the source of all our misfortune. If we were to have any hope of salvation, it was the only way.' He paused and closed his eyes. Had he just grown weary, or was his time here drawing to an end?

But he opened his eyes again. 'I did not confide this secret to my men. Only the boatswain knew it. He made sure the foredeck was deserted, and when the captain disappeared into his cabin, I set to work. The plug was easily removed. The doubloons were packed in rolls of sixty coins apiece. It took me no more than ten minutes to jettison all twenty-five rolls.'

The first mate closed his eyes again. Talking seemed to be tiring him now, but his voice was still firm and resonant.

'As ill fortune would have it, one of the captain's men had seen me at work on the figurehead,' he went on, 'and reported it to him. He was naturally eager to know where I had hidden the gold, the avaricious fool. He believed to the last that I'd hidden it – he found it inconceivable that I could have cast fifteen hundred doubloons into the sea. There was simply no place in his head for the notion that the gold was lost. It will lie at the bottom of the ocean for evermore.'

The first mate fell silent, his eyes still closed.

'The gold is at the bottom of the ocean, you say?'

Belper! He had climbed on to the ship unnoticed and was glaring at the first mate, purple in the face with rage. Even his bald head was flushed. Suddenly he yelled, 'You swine! Give me back my doubloons!' And he came charging towards the sailor.

Vicki and Peter acted as one.

Vicki hurled herself at Belper's left leg, Peter at his right. They hung on with all their might, bringing him to the ground. He hit the deck with an almighty crash.

For a moment Vicki felt the man's leg muscles go limp, but then he began to kick far harder than she'd expected. Peter, lying beside her, was also shaken this way and that. She noticed that, while trying to kick himself free, Belper was inching along the deck towards the first mate. 'You swine!' he yelled again.

Vicki continued to cling to his leg. She hung on with every ounce of strength she possessed, determined not to be shaken off at any price. She shut her eyes. Hang on, she told herself, hang on, but she could tell that Belper was still making progress. Then she heard a dull *thud*, and this time his legs stayed limp.

Without letting go, she opened her eyes and looked up.

Phil was standing there.

It really *was* Phil, looking thoroughly ferocious and brandishing some kind of club.

'Did he hurt you?'

Vicki sat up. Belper was lying face down on the deck, inert and unconscious. 'Not us,' she said. 'He wasn't after us, he was going to . . .'

The first mate!

But he had disappeared.

Vicki looked around. The corpses on the deck had also vanished, and all she could see where the dead captain had lain were clean, bare planks.

Peter had sat up too. Now he got to his feet. He looked down at Belper, then turned to Phil. 'Great job. I think you saved this guy's life.'

'Saved his life? How do you mean?'

'If he'd reached the first mate, I reckon it wouldn't have done him any good. Belper, I mean.'

Phil surveyed the deck. 'What first mate?'

It turned out that the whole of the *Storm Goddess*'s crew had vanished by the time Phil had climbed aboard. He wasn't sorry. 'What I heard from down below was quite enough for me.' He raised his head. 'Speaking of sounds, can you hear it, too, that funny noise?'

They could indeed. It sounded as if the timbers were creaking and groaning, as if the ship herself were sighing. Vicki thought she could feel the deck moving beneath her feet. 'The first mate said we should leave the ship quickly when he disappeared, so come on, let's go!'

'What about him?' Peter asked, and pointed to Belper. 'Do we leave him here?'

Belper moaned and struggled into a sitting position. Then he just sat there glassy-eyed, staring into space. He didn't utter a word.

The ship's timbers were creaking and groaning more loudly now, and there was no doubt that the deck was moving. Something was happening to the *Storm Goddess*.

'Hey, Mr Belper,' said Peter, 'we've got to get off. And in a hurry.'

No answer. Belper continued staring into space.

'What do we do now?' Phil asked. He looked across at the rope ladder hanging from the bulwark.

Vicki and Peter gripped Belper's arms, and – lo and behold – he struggled to his feet. But he simply stood there looking dazed, until they gave his arms a tug and he came to life. They led him over to the ladder like an obedient child. Luckily he was capable of climbing down the ladder unaided. At the bottom he once more stood there like a stuffed dummy, so the three of them shepherded him outside the fence, where he could come to no harm.

The *Storm Goddess* was breaking up.

More precisely, she was collapsing. The masts subsided into her hull. The sails crumbled to dust in no time at all. The hull disintegrated, too, and the wood could actually be seen rotting and decomposing. In the meantime, the *Storm Goddess*'s creaks, groans and sighs rang out across the mud flats. But they sounded contented rather than agonized – at least to Vicki's ears.

She stood beside Phil and Peter and watched as the ship became, within minutes, what she should by rights have been a long time ago: an eighteenth-century square-rigged sailing ship that had sunk in a storm and lain on the sea bed for two hundred and thirty years before being injudiciously exposed to the air.

They stood there listening to the creaks and sighs, which grew steadily fainter until they died away altogether.

The *Storm Goddess* had become an earth-coloured mound. Although the mound was cigar-shaped, no one would have recognized it as the remains of a ship. It wasn't wood any more, just a substance almost indistinguishable from the mud around it.

'Goodbye, *Storm Goddess*,' Vicki said softly.

She was feeling a little sad.

More than a little sad, to be honest.

But the *Storm Goddess* and her crew were at peace. It had taken a lot of luck, Vicki reflected, because the whole thing could have gone terribly wrong.

Suddenly Peter said, 'The packet with the journal in it!' He looked around. 'Where is it?'

Even as he asked the question, he realized, like Vicki, that the packet also must have vanished. He knew exactly where it had been lying, but there was nothing to be seen there but mud.

Belper, still looking dazed, was standing where they had left him.

A siren started wailing in the distance, and the police car came racing across the mud flats with the harbour master and Grogan and Willis on board.

Closely following the police car was another vehicle. It pulled up beside the fence, and out jumped Rose Redd, who hurried towards them through the gate in the fence.

Slowly, the harbour master got out of the police car and walked over to the mound of earth that had been the *Storm Goddess*. He gazed at it with the same dumbfounded expression he must have worn when first confronted by the ship that had mysteriously materialized out of the eighteenth century. Then he shook his head and turned away. He aimed a deliberately casual glance at Belper, who was standing beside the fence on his own, but subjected Vicki and Peter to a long, menacing stare.

Rose, on the other hand, he favoured with an ingratiating smile. 'I've got him eating out of my hand,' she whispered to Vicki and Peter when she reached them. 'He thinks I know he was planning to go half shares with Belper – which I do. Don't let him intimidate you.'

Certainly not, thought Vicki. Not after all she'd been through. Compared with his ancestor the captain, the harbour master seemed no more than a harmless pantomime ogre.

'Well,' Rose went on, 'I can forget my article on the *Storm Goddess*'s hidden treasure.' She eyed the mound of earth ruefully. 'The gold's gone, I imagine.'

'It always was,' said Vicki. 'The first mate threw it overboard.'

'Really?' Rose looked back at the harbour master. 'So all his crooked dealings were a complete waste of time.' She indicated Belper, who was standing motionless beside the fence. 'What happened to him?'

'He got a bang on the head,' Vicki said quickly. 'Up on deck somewhere. We've no idea how he did it.' She avoided Peter's eye. 'He should really go to casualty.'

'I'll take care of that,' said Rose. 'Tell me all about it later, OK?' When Vicki nodded, Rose turned to go, then stopped short. 'Tell me, does your father still want to buy the Seashell?'

'Of course he does. Always has.'

'Hmm,' was all Rose said. She hurried over to Belper, led him to her car, and drove off with him.

'Thanks, Vicki,' said Phil.

'You're welcome.'

In the meantime, people had been streaming out across the mud flats on foot. Nearly all the townsfolk had been roused from their beds – the *Storm Goddess*'s creaks and groans had seen to that. The gate in the fence was still open, so it wasn't long before they were crowding round the mound of earth that had once been a ship. Like the harbour master, they seemed even more disconcerted by this development than they had been by the ship's appearance four days ago. Their buzz of conversation and the hum of the generators combined to create quite a racket.

'Shall we go?' Peter asked.

'I'm wondering whether to open for business,' said Phil. 'This could be the ideal—' He broke off and cocked his head. 'What's that noise?'

'Just the crowd, I should think,' said Peter.

'No, no.' Phil shook his head. 'Come on, let's go and see.' Taking each one by the arm, he led them a little way across the mud flats.

Vicki could now hear it, too.

A sound like rushing water.

And then, far away, at the mouth of the bay, where the open sea began, she saw something glitter in the moonlight.

Vicki waited awhile, and the glitter intensified.

She breathed a sigh of relief.

The sea was on its way back.

PART THREE
THE SEASHELL ROOM

TWENTY

The bay was dry no longer.

The tide rose and fell the way it should, and the *Bay Gazette* reported that the shellfish population was recovering with remarkable speed. The channel leading to the harbour was in constant use, and old Captain Ahab and his band were once more marching across the mud flats at low tide. Holidaymakers with rucksacks roamed the shore, and little children splashed around, screeching with delight, in the pools of black sludge.

Although the cigar-shaped mound in the middle of the bay still protruded above the surface at low water, the waves had already flattened it considerably. Another week or two, and it would disappear altogether.

Three days after its sudden disintegration, the mysterious

ship that had lain there ceased to be featured in the press or on TV. There were more newsworthy items than reports and pictures of something that no longer existed.

Of course, great excitement had reigned the night the sea had returned. The bay hadn't filled up in a flash – the spectators had been able to withdraw to the safety of the beach – but the tide had risen so quickly that it proved impossible to salvage the fence, the portable toilets, the floodlights, the generator, or the police camper van. The fire department took care of that at low tide the next day, but most of the equipment had naturally been ruined by sea water.

Only Phil's trailer remained intact. He had persuaded his uncle to tow it back to the beach with his police car, and he'd even managed to take most of his tables with him.

Vicki was having breakfast.

It was Monday, a rest day, and more than a week had elapsed since the *Storm Goddess's* disappearance. Eileen had gone off to do some shopping, and Dad would be out for the morning – 'on official business', he'd proclaimed with a mysterious air. He thought Vicki didn't know what he was up to, and she'd feigned ignorance rather than spoil his surprise. If all went well, he'd said, he would have an important announcement to make, so her party this afternoon was perfectly timed.

Vicki had invited her friends – the ones who had shared the secret of the *Storm Goddess* – to a little celebration in the Seashell Restaurant. The *Storm Goddess*'s figurehead was coming home!

Mr Pacino, the little man in the beret and the painter's smock, had restored the head and would be reinstalling it this afternoon. He had already done some preparatory work on the base the previous Monday. A ladder had sufficed for that job, but today some scaffolding was required, and the men from the scaffolding company had already put it up.

Vicki took a bite of buttered toast.

Not only was today the day of the *Storm Goddess*'s return, but today would also be the day Vicki put Dadon the spot. For ten days now, her unspoken question – 'How much did *you* know?' – had hung in the air between them. But if she wanted him to answer it, she herself would have to answer a question from *him*. A highly unpleasant question: 'How did *you* know?'

But first another question needed answering: when had her father stopped being a fan of the *Storm Goddess*, and why?

Abruptly, Vicki abandoned her slice of toast and jumped up. Before she could change her mind, she darted out of the restaurant, along the hall, and up two flights of stairs to the attic. Quickly, she unlocked the door and went in.

That was where the first mate had sat and gazed at her with his back propped against the old trunk. She could recall the apparition in such vivid detail, she knew she would never forget it as long as she lived. At the same time, it now all seemed so unlikely that she found it almost impossible to believe she had actually seen it.

She opened the trunk.

Before long she had lifted out the last of the files and brought to light the folders that covered the bottom of the trunk. Laying aside the one inscribed in pencil with her father's name and 'Lower Fourth', she removed the one marked 'Upper Fourth' and opened it.

Like the other folder, it contained some drawings. Dad had drawn one sailing ship after another, sometimes in the harbour, sometimes on the high seas, sometimes in a storm, sometimes becalmed, but always the *Storm Goddess*.

There were other drawings too, of course. Like Vicki's art teacher, her father's art teacher also must have said, 'Today I want you to draw the kinds of things you see on a beach,' or words to that effect. But whenever Dad had been allowed to draw whatever he wanted, the inevitable result was yet another *Storm Goddess*.

Vicki took out the folder marked 'Lower Fifth' and started leafing through it.

More *Storm Goddess*es, one after another. She shook her head, amazed that he hadn't become bored with the subject. She turned over the next sheet.

And stared at it transfixed.

Seashells!

The whole sheet was covered with drawings of seashells. All kinds: large and small, smooth and fluted, white and coloured, long and round. Big clamshells, little mussel shells, tiny cockleshells.

And all of them, Vicki saw at once, were represented downstairs in the restaurant.

Had the art teacher said, 'Today we're going to draw the shells on the walls of the Seashell Restaurant'? It seemed unlikely. Vicki turned over some more sheets. One seashell picture after another.

No more drawings of the *Storm Goddess*.

She turned back to the first seashell picture. It bore her father's name with 'Lower Fifth' below it. But there was something else. It was a date: 'November 1975.'

None of the other drawings had been dated.

Vicki stared into space.

Quickly, she replaced the folder in the chest with the other two, tossed the files in after them, shut the trunk and the door of the attic, and hurried downstairs to her bedroom, where she immediately dialled Gran's number on her mobile. 'I'm not available right now,' she heard, 'but you can leave a message after the tone.' If Gran had turned off her mobile, she really wasn't available. Vicki ran down the stairs and fetched her bike from the shed.

It took her less than five minutes to get to the church-yard gate.

And less than a minute to reach Grandpa's grave. Carved on the gravestone were the words: *Lost at sea, November 1975.*

Vicki entered the restaurant to find her father seated at a table near the counter.

He regarded her in silence. 'I went to look at Grandpa's grave,' she said. 'He was drowned at sea in November 1975. That's the same date as—' She broke off.

'As the one you found on my first seashell drawing,' said her father.

She stared at him.

'By the way,' he went on, 'before I forget, you can keep the journal. It belongs to you now.'

She had to sit down. 'Th-thanks,' she stammered. He'd known *everything*. 'So you knew everything,' she said aloud.

He shook his head. 'Certainly not everything, but some of it.' He looked at her. 'Something was obviously both-ering you. I'd be a pretty poor parent if I hadn't spotted that, and noticed that strange things were going on in this building – things that seemed to have some connection with what was happening out in the bay. Or the other way around.'

'But why didn't you ever say anything? Why didn't you stop me?'

Her father looked over at the captain's portrait on the wall. 'I came close to it more than once. But I knew that if I did, if I interfered, you wouldn't have been able to do what you had to do.' He looked back at her. 'On the other hand, it *was* a dangerous business. I found it extremely difficult *not* to interfere, believe me.'

Vicki got up and gave him a hug.

After a while, she asked, 'But why did you become a seashell fan?' She could imagine why, but she wanted to hear it from his own lips.

He stared into space for a moment. 'I always missed my father terribly when he was far away at sea – that's why I dreamed of going to sea myself. Drawing the *Storm Goddess* was my way of making that dream come true.' He paused. 'But then my father was drowned. The sea became his grave, so I didn't want to go to sea any more. I mean, who wants to sail around on his father's grave?' His eyes roamed over the seashell-covered walls. 'But I still dreamed of going to far-off places.'

Vicki nodded. 'So you picked a subject that would let you do so without going to sea.'

'The South Seas, the Indian Ocean – when I drew those shells, I could go anywhere in my imagination.' He looked at her. 'And I've always wanted my daughter to do the same.'

Silence fell. After a while, Vicki said, 'But I won't be sailing around on *my* father's grave if *I* go to sea.'

'You're right.' Her father smiled. 'I've grasped that at last, with a little help from the Storm Goddess.'

Mr Pacino and the Storm Goddess were running late, not that this delayed the celebration in the Seashell. There was plenty to talk about and tons to eat and drink. Eileen had baked a mountain of pastries, and Vicki had made an equally mountainous pile of sandwiches. The liquid refreshments included orange juice and lemonade and, for those who wanted it and were old enough, some genuine French champagne.

'At my age,' Gran declared, 'a glass of champagne can't hurt. Better still, a couple of glasses.' She was wearing a pair of glitzy Indian earrings and had even cancelled her Monday-night gathering.

Phil had an announcement. He had pulled it off at last: he'd managed to obtain permission to set up his fish and chip stand in a new spot. 'In the future,' he said triumphantly, 'my customers won't have to eat their cod and chips *behind* the lifeboats. They can enjoy them on the beach *in front* of it, with a nice view of the bay!' Everyone congratulated him.

'But,' said Vicki, 'I thought you couldn't get permission before because the beach is protected.'

'It still is, but the ban doesn't apply to *mobile* snack stands.' Phil grinned. 'I've simply left the wheels on.'

Rose turned to Vicki. 'You asked me a question once, remember?'

Vicki nodded.

'Well? What do you think? What's the answer?'

Vicki looked at her. 'Your name really is Rose Redd.'

'Bingo.' Rose nodded approvingly. 'Anyone born with a name like mine either changes it or embraces it.'

Peter asked her how Belper was.

'He's doing fine,' Rose said. 'The hospital's discharging him tomorrow, I hear.'

'Is he really better?' asked Phil.

'Absolutely,' said Rose. 'It was concussion. Someone on board that ship clonked him on the head. Whoever did it deserves a medal,' she added.

Phil assumed an air of innocent interest.

'But he can't remember a thing about it.'

'Nothing?'

'Nothing at all. There's a gap in his memory between the time he arrived in this town and waking up in the hospital. The doctor says he's suffering from systematic amnesia.'

'From what?' asked Eileen.

'Systematic amnesia. It's a kind of memory loss that only applies to certain events. In Belper's case, that means anything to do with his search for the gold.'

'Oh, sure,' said Peter, 'if he could remember *that*, he'd go raving mad.'

When the laughter had died down, Vicki's father cleared his throat, gaining everyone's attention. 'Well,' he said, 'I think it's time I told you all my big surprise.'

Vicki took a surreptitious look around. Nobody seemed to suspect a thing aside from her and Rose, who was smiling as if she not only had guessed what Dad was going to say but knew it perfectly well.

He got up and went over to the serving counter, where he'd left his chef's hat. Having put it on his head, he said, 'I've an announcement to make in my capacity as chef and leaseholder of the Seashell Restaurant.' He paused briefly. 'Or rather, ex-leaseholder.'

'*Ex*-leaseholder?' Gran frowned. 'Don't tell me you're giving up the restaurant?'

'On the contrary,' he said. He took a folder from the

300

counter, removed a document, and opened it at the last page. Then he held it up so everyone could see. It bore some signatures and a fat red seal.

Eileen was the first to catch on. 'No!' she cried. 'I don't believe it! You mean the Seashell belongs to you?'

He nodded slowly and solemnly. 'I've bought the place. The deal was finalized this morning.'

'Hooray!' shouted Vicki. She hadn't been as sure as she'd thought. She shouted even louder. 'Hooray!'

'Congratulations,' said Peter, raising his glass.

They all clinked their glasses, and it was like New Year's Eve but even nicer.

When calm had returned, Eileen said, 'I'd like to know why the harbour master wanted to sell all of a sudden.'

'It wasn't a question of *wanting* to,' said Vicki's father. 'A certain lady gave him a bit of a nudge. How, I'm not too sure.'

All eyes turned to Rose.

'Well,' she said, 'surely you can guess?' She surveyed the expectant faces around her. 'OK, I'll tell you, but you mustn't breathe a word or my editor will fire me.'

Everyone nodded.

'The night I was working on my article about the treasure hidden on board the *Storm Goddess* – the night the ship disappeared – the harbour master suddenly called me.

He hemmed and hawed to start with. Then he asked if Belper had told me anything. I got the message at once. I said he had. I also hinted that I knew he'd planned to go half shares with Belper. 'The man's lying,' he said, so I told him a blatant lie of my own: I said that Belper had given me a sworn statement for publication in case the harbour master tried to swindle him. Strangely enough, he swallowed my story on the spot.'

'Nothing strange about it,' said Phil. 'I heard Belper threaten him. He said he'd taken out some insurance.'

'So that's why the harbour master caved so easily.' Rose gave a contented nod. 'He was scared I'd publish the statement and he'd be run out of office.'

'Well?' said Eileen. '*Will* you publish it?'

Rose shook her head. 'No, I can't any more – not now. I made a deal with him: I wouldn't publish it if he sold the Seashell Restaurant.'

'You really did that?' Eileen said incredulously.

Rose nodded.

'But why?' asked Eileen. 'I mean, why would you do such a thing? What's . . . er . . . in it for you?'

Rose smiled. 'You think I've got designs on your boss or something?'

Eileen turned puce.

'Don't worry,' said Rose, 'the harbour master's my only

302

concern.' She looked around the table. 'And what I'm going to say now may surprise you: he isn't such a bad harbour master, all things considered, not really. Take the way he turned the *Storm Goddess* into a tourist attraction; *that* showed plenty of initiative.' She paused. 'Unfortunately, he's also a selfish, unscrupulous money-grubber, so he needs careful watching. And believe me, I'm going to watch him like a hawk from now on.'

There wasn't a person in the room who doubted it.

'Talk about a money-grubber,' said Vicki's father, 'the harbour master didn't let this place go for peanuts, as you can imagine. I've had to take out a whopping mortgage.' He smiled, first at Eileen and then at Vicki. 'Still, we'll manage.'

At that moment, someone knocked on the door of the restaurant.

Little Mr Pacino was standing outside.

TWENTY-ONE

They all clustered round the scaffolding as Mr Pacino opened the crate he'd made to fit the Storm Goddess's head, lined with padding to protect it. 'I can only repeat,' he said, 'that at more than two centuries old, this carving is a real treasure.' Carefully, he lifted out the head and deposited it on a blanket fetched by Vicki. 'Well, here she is.'

There lay the Storm Goddess. It was she, sure enough, but she'd undergone a startling change. What was so different about her? Mr Pacino had naturally replaced the paint that had flaked off her right eye. He had also filled the cavity in her head, leaving a hole for the new plug he'd already inserted into the base. Looking at the Storm Goddess, Vicki finally realized what was so startlingly different about her: her colours glowed. They glowed as if they'd been painted only yesterday.

'I've cleaned every square inch of her head,' said Mr Pacino. 'And I've preserved her, too, of course. The harbour master will be getting a big fat bill from me.'

Vicki's father sighed. 'You'd better send the bill to me, I'm afraid.' The restorer looked at him enquiringly. 'I've just bought this place, complete with fixtures and fittings. That includes the head and the seashells, of course. The harbour master was generous enough to throw in his ancestor's portrait as well.'

'So you've bought the place at last. Congratulations!' Mr Pacino seemed genuinely delighted. 'In that case, I'll have another look at the bill. Now, let's put the lady back.' He turned to Vicki. 'Like to give me a hand again?'

'You bet.'

Mr Pacino replaced the head in its crate and secured the lid, which had a ring in the centre. He produced a rope from his bag and tied one end to the ring. 'Would you mind climbing up and taking the other end with you? Take the blanket as well.'

Vicki climbed up the ladder in no time, followed by Mr Pacino. Together, they hauled the crate on to the platform, hand over hand. Mr Pacino lifted out the head and laid it down on the blanket. 'You take the right side, I'll take the left,' he told Vicki. 'Grip it by the chin and the hair.'

Slowly, they lifted the head until it was directly above the plug. 'Now lower it gently,' said Mr Pacino. 'Yes, that's right.' He turned the head a fraction and said, 'Done.' He and Vicki stepped aside. Everyone at the foot of the scaffolding applauded.

The Storm Goddess was back in the Seashell Restaurant.

Vicki and Mr Pacino lowered the crate to the floor and climbed down after it.

'The next job you should tackle,' Mr Pacino said to Vicki's father, 'is those seashells.' He went over to the wall and tapped one of the big clamshells with his knuckles. It sounded hollow, but it rattled as well. 'They're loose and in need of restoration, like I told you. Don't leave it too long.'

'One thing at a time. First I must catch my breath financially.'

'I was only mentioning it.' Having stowed the rope in his bag and picked up the empty crate, Mr Pacino looked up at the Storm Goddess and gave a satisfied nod. His eyes strayed across the seashell-encrusted walls and came to rest on the captain's portrait. 'Are you really going to leave that picture hanging there? It's completely worthless from an artistic point of view, and I doubt if it bears any resemblance to the man it was supposed to portray.'

'It's staying,' said Vicki, very firmly.

Her father glanced at her in surprise, but then he nodded just as firmly.

'Fair enough,' said Mr Pacino. 'Well, renewed congratulations and have a nice day, everyone.' And he made his exit.

They all sat down again, and the celebration in the restaurant continued.

Peter reached for another sandwich. 'Seafood isn't really my thing,' he remarked to Phil, 'but I can't think of another place where you can get such delicious fish and chips. What gave you the idea?'

'Yes,' said Gran, 'I'd like to know that too.'

'It was like this,' said Phil, and he proceeded to tell them the story of the little girl who'd turned up at his snack bar shortly after it opened and asked for some fish and proper chips. 'And all I had was hot dogs, burgers and French fries.'

Vicki was staring at the captain's portrait. No resemblance, phooey! His face had looked *just* like that: not smooth, but pitted, as if the sea had eaten it away. He hadn't been smiling on board the ship the way he was in the picture. His smile had a malign, contemptuous quality. This was because in the picture, his eyes weren't smiling like his lips, but were narrowed in an ominous way. The captain's evil, mocking smile was directed at the opposite wall – at the spot where the Storm Goddess had been replaced.

Wait a minute . . . what had been there before? The unoccupied base, of course. But what was beneath the base? What had been there *before* the Storm Goddess's head was installed in the restaurant?

Seashells.

When the captain's portrait had first been hung, the opposite wall – the wall he was gazing at – had been an expanse of seashells.

The captain had been gazing at them. Gazing at them with an evil, mocking, almost diabolical smile, as if he knew a secret no one else would ever fathom.

Vicki recalled what the first mate had said: 'At the same time, this hiding place was in the nature of a cruel jest on the captain's part. It was a special place – one that all could see without ever suspecting what it concealed.'

And she could see the words in his journal:

The captain has hidden the gold away, but I believe I am too well acquainted with his way of thinking not to be able to guess its whereabouts. . . .

She thought some more. The first mate had been refer-ring to the hiding place on board the *Storm Goddess* . . . but there was something else in his journal – something she hadn't registered at first . . . the chests! The chests the captain had made his men carry ashore. The townsfolk had thought they seemed exceptionally heavy. Could they have . . . ?

'A *cruel jest on the captain's part* . . . '

'The seashells!' cried Vicki.

Everyone stared at her.

She jumped up. 'The chests the captain brought ashore, there may have been more in them than seashells!'

'Vicki, what's the matter with you?'

Heedless of her father's worried face, she darted over to the big clamshell Mr Pacino had tapped on earlier – the one that had sounded hollow but had rattled as well. 'I need something with a sharp point,' she called out. 'A steak knife will do.' She looked around, but nobody moved. 'In the sideboard!' She was about to make a dash for it, but Peter got there first. He pulled open a drawer and came hurrying over to her with a steak knife in his hand. 'Take it easy,' he said. 'If there's anything under there, it won't run away.'

Vicki shot him a look of gratitude and started digging at the plaster around the rim of the shell. She worked quickly but with care.

Her father came over. 'What are you doing, Vicki? Hey, you'll make a mess of that shell! Stop it! What's got into you? I—' He broke off.

She finished loosening the shell and took it off the wall.

As she did so, something fell to the floor.

It landed with a hard, metallic sound. The hard, metallic noise persisted as it bounced a couple of times and finally came to rest.

There it lay.

As bright and shiny as if it had been minted only yesterday.

None of them had ever seen one before.

But they all knew at once what it was.

The thing that lay there was a gold coin.

It was long past midnight, and Vicki was all by herself in the restaurant, listening to the murmur of the sea. To the familiar, reassuring murmur of the waves breaking on the shore. Unable to sleep, she had crept quietly downstairs and was now sitting, with her feet tucked up on the chair beneath her, at table nineteen, the small, secluded table near the counter that gave a good view of the restaurant.

She hadn't turned any lights on. There was plenty of light coming through the windows – not moonlight, because the moon was new, but from the street lights on the road along the quay. It was bright enough for Vicki to make out the Storm Goddess's eyes from where she sat.

The scaffolding was still in place. The scaffolders had been scheduled to take it down that evening, but Dad had called the firm and put them off. There was no hurry, because the restaurant was going to remain closed for the time being.

After discovering the first gold coin, Vicki had, with Peter's help, removed another five shells, altogether different ones in altogether different places, and more gold coins had come to light beneath all five. They were Spanish doubloons dating from the eighteenth century. Summoned back by telephone, Mr Pacino had excitedly confirmed this and delivered a brief but impassioned lecture on the subject. He explained that 'doubloon' was a generic term applied to various gold pieces, and that these six coins were 'onzas', also known as 'quadruples,' each of which was worth sixteen silver piastres, that is eight escudos, or four pistoles. And they, he went on, had been the most valuable doubloons of all.

Mr Pacino had said he wasn't qualified to estimate the coins' current value, but if he erred on the cautious side and assumed that roughly a third of the shells concealed doubloons, the hoard must be worth a substantial amount. A very substantial amount – in fact, it made his head spin even to hazard a guess at their potential value.

In answer to a query from Eileen, he had delivered a

further brief lecture on points of law. According to him, half of such a hoard belonged to its discoverer and half to its owner. From the legal standpoint, therefore, Vicki owned half of the gold coins, and her father the other half. Moreover, the treasure trove was something that had lain hidden for so long that its original ownership had lapsed.

Rose asked Vicki what she had meant when she said there might have been more than seashells in the chests the captain had brought ashore.

So Vicki fetched the first mate's journal from her room and read aloud from it:

'The captain came as a passenger aboard a cotton-carrying merchantman that anchored in the harbour not far from the Gertrude. He had himself rowed ashore together with two dark-skinned men attired in colourful, outlandish clothes. The townsfolk marvelled at these men.

'They marvelled likewise when the captain had several mysterious chests brought ashore. These chests seemed exceptionally heavy. What, everyone wondered, could be concealed in them?'

Vicki shut the book with a snap. 'In other words, the chests held more than the seashells he and his two assistants used to decorate the walls of this room. The chests also contained the gold pieces they hid beneath the shells.'

'But how did he come by the gold?' Eileen asked.

'Probably by trading in slaves,' said Peter. 'My guess is, the slave ship he captured with the *Storm Goddess* wasn't the only one. I think he'd done the same with other ships in the past.'

Later on, when all the excitement had subsided and Rose, Gran and Phil had departed – when Eileen was clearing away the remains of the celebration in the kitchen and Dad was in his office discussing the forthcoming restoration of the Seashell Restaurant with Mr Pacino – Vicki and Peter had spent a long time sitting together at table nineteen: *their* table.

'This treasure business blows your mind,' Peter said, shaking his head. 'It'll take a while to sink in.'

Vicki couldn't help laughing. 'The *Storm Goddess* business was pretty mind-blowing, but we managed to handle that.'

'We did,' said Peter, nodding. Silence fell. Then he said, 'Vicki, I talked to my parents, but they won't budge. We're leaving on Thursday.'

'Thursday?'

'At least I don't live *so* far away.' He adjusted his glasses with his forefinger. 'I've already found out the best way to get here by train.'

'Or I could come to visit you. Besides,' said Vicki, 'we've

still got a few days, and we can do a lot together in a few days. A *whole* lot.'

And that, she reflected now, as she sat in the restaurant long after midnight, was the plain truth. The *Storm Goddess* business had lasted only a few days, but it couldn't be denied that she and Peter had done plenty together in that time.

Vicki looked up at the Storm Goddess.

She still gazed down into the restaurant, just as she had before her restoration, since the base still slanted forward a little.

But she was no longer looking at Vicki.

Vicki had noticed this earlier, when she'd climbed down the ladder after helping to reinstall the head, but it hadn't surprised her. After all, Mr Pacino had deprived the Storm Goddess of her squint by replacing the missing flake of paint on her right eye.

Never mind, thought Vicki. She would put that right the first chance she got. She would climb up and scratch a little paint off the right eye. Then the Storm Goddess would squint once more and look at her in the same old way.

No time like the present, she thought. The scaffolding was still in place. She only had to get up, go over, and climb the ladder.

But she didn't move.

The Storm Goddess was looking down into the room with an earnest, tight-lipped expression, as if she had secrets to guard.

But she didn't have any left, not now.

She had surrendered all her secrets so as to save the crew of the ship she protected.

Vicki called to her across the restaurant, 'You did a good job, Storm Goddess.'

And as she said that, and heard herself saying it, she realized that it was a farewell.

She was saying goodbye to the head of a figurehead that had been washed up on the shore a long time ago.

A very long time ago.